"Hello?" she said again. "Come on out—I saw you earlier. Let me help."

Nothing. Melinda listened a moment longer, then bent to retrieve her notebook with a sigh. She had seen a ghost, that much she knew, and so much for her hopes of getting through this estate sale ghost-free. Clearly this was one of the shy ones who would have to be coaxed out before she could help it cross over.

Melinda straightened and looked straight into an angry white face. The wide pale eyes stretched and the mouth gaped and drooled. Wild hair squirmed and twisted. Two clawed hands reached for Melinda's neck with cold fingers. They trailed white cobwebs.

"Leave!" the mouth wailed. *"Run!"*

The strength drained from Melinda's knees. Every animal instinct shouted at her to run, but she couldn't. Fear rooted her feet, made them heavy. Like a bird watching an approaching snake, she stared into the ghost's oozing face.

"Go!" it screeched.

Also available from Pocket Books

Ghost Whisperer: Revenge

Coming soon

Ghost Whisperer: Ghost Trap

GHOST WHISPERER™

Based on the hit TV series created by

JOHN GRAY

PLAGUE ROOM

STEVEN PIZIKS

POCKET STAR BOOKS

New York   London   Toronto   Sydney

Pocket Star Books
A Division of Simon & Schuster, Inc.
1230 Avenue of the Americas
New York, NY 10020.

This book is a work of fiction. Names, characters, places, and incidents either are products of the author's imagination or are used fictitiously. Any resemblance to actual events or locales or persons, living or dead, is entirely coincidental.

First Pocket Star Books paperback edition December 2008

POCKET STAR BOOKS and colophon are registered trademarks of Simon & Schuster, Inc.

For information about special discounts for bulk purchases, please contact Simon & Schuster Special Sales at 1-800-456-6798 or business@simonandschuster.com.

Cover design by Richard Yoo

Manufactured in the United States of America

10 9 8 7 6 5 4 3 2 1

ISBN-13: 978-1-4165-6015-9
ISBN-10:   1-4165-6015-7

To Randy

Historian's Note

The following story takes place during the first season of *Ghost Whisperer*.

1

A WHITE DRESS SHIRT whipped through the air. Melinda Gordon ducked. The shirt missed her and wrapped itself around Jack Perry's head. He gave a muffled scream and clawed at his face, trying to pull it off. Melinda leaped forward to help him. She hooked her fingers under the collar and pulled.

"Stop this!" she shouted at empty air. Her heart pounded with fear and exertion. "You have to stop!"

The shirt blurred Jack's features, making him look like a Halloween ghost. Melinda yanked hard. The shirt came away with a soft tearing sound, a bandage coming off an old wound. Jack sucked in a deep breath. Behind him, racks of plastic-wrapped clothes rustled and sighed among themselves, filling the dry cleaning store with angry whispers. Melinda tensed, wondering if any more of them would fly out at them. Her fingers clutched at the shirt. A red dress lifted from the rack in a ghastly parody of a dance, hissing in its plastic wrapping. Melinda grabbed a pair of scissors from the counter and brandished them, but the dress staggered and collapsed in stages to the floor, the plastic billowing out like a half-dead balloon. The dry cleaning store fell silent.

Jack, his face pale, leaned panting against the service counter. He stared at Melinda for a long moment. Shreds of white cloth hung in his curly brown hair. He had a slight build that combined with pointed, boyish features and green eyes to give him an air Melinda could only think of as elfin.

"You said you can help."

"Usually I can." Melinda set the scissors down and brushed back a lock of long dark hair. Her features were smooth, and her chin came to a rounded point that her husband Jim assured her was extremely cute. She wore a flowing white blouse that set off an almost porcelain complexion. "Are you sure you don't know anything about the ghost? I can't help a spirit cross over until I know what's keeping it here. It would help if I even had a name or a gender."

"If I knew anything, I'd tell you," Jack said in exasperation. "It's been like this for a month now, and I have no freaking—hello!"

Melinda blinked at him, then realized he was looking at someone behind her and turned around. A tall, redheaded woman was standing in the doorway. She wore a low-cut yellow blouse, and a matching embroidered skirt of raw silk clung to her thighs. No one would have called her beautiful—her face was a little too long, her eyes a bit too small, and Melinda thought she really needed to wear her hair down instead of in that French twist. But the look Jack gave her was the same look a hungry artist reserved for a Botticelli painting or a Michelangelo sculpture. Or the one Melinda sometimes gave Jim when he wasn't looking.

"Hello, Jack," the woman said, stepping into the store. Her voice was startlingly low, a wax comb dripping with honey. "Is my party dress ready?"

"Yeah! Sure thing, Polly." Jack eagerly thumbed a switch, and the rack moved its load of clothes smoothly through the area behind the counter. Melinda held her breath, waiting to see if anything would leap free. She half hoped something would— she might see the ghost responsible—even though she knew it would be hard to explain to Polly.

Jack plucked a plastic-sheathed black dress from the rack and held it up. "Here it is. All set."

"I'm impressed," Polly said with a small smile. "You didn't even ask to see my ticket."

"I—I remembered your number," Jack said. He looked oddly flustered. His face colored, and his gaze darted nervously down to his hands, then back at Polly. "Anyway, it's all set. Oh—one of the buttons was coming loose. I sewed it back on for you. No extra charge."

Polly cocked her head. "Thanks. Service like that will keep me coming back."

"It's why we—I—do it," Jack said with a painfully shy smile. Melinda, standing in the corner, flicked her gaze around the shop, watching, waiting. The spirit was around here somewhere. It had to be. She could feel its cold, confused eyes staring at her. It was afraid and it was angry, and that made it dangerous. Living people did terrible things out of fear and anger. The dead were less restrained and often did much worse.

Polly took a pink leather wallet from her pocket and paid the dry cleaning check. Jack fidgeted during the transaction. He clearly wanted to say more, but felt too shy. Polly accepted her change, and Melinda saw her hand brush Jack's. His eyes widened just a little.

"Is there something else?" Polly asked. Her expression was open and guileless, inviting. Even hopeful.

Jack swallowed. He seemed to have forgotten Melinda entirely. Polly waited, holding the dress folded neatly over one arm. Melinda, for her part, found herself getting caught up in the drama unfolding before her. She watched from her corner, trying to remain the unobtrusive outsider.

"I . . . I . . ." Jack said.

Polly leaned forward. Melinda held her breath. "Yes?" Polly asked.

"I . . . forgot to give you your change." Jack slapped the cash register and it opened with a bang. Quickly he counted out a few coins and dropped them into Polly's hand. "Sorry."

"Oh," she said, her disappointment clear. "Thanks."

Polly turned to go. Melinda started to speak up, then caught herself. Anything she said would only embarrass both of them. But Jack looked so unhappy and Polly so disappointed. It didn't seem fair or right. Except there were times when it was best to interfere and times when it was best to bow out. The trick was telling the difference between the two.

"Hey, Polly," Jack called out suddenly.

Polly turned, holding the dress before her like a shield. "Yes?"

"I . . . I . . ." Jack seemed to lose his nerve for a moment. Then words burst out of him in a rush. "I'll bet you look great in that." He flushed deeply. Melinda could see how much the words had cost him, and she held back a little sigh of relief. They were talking again. Things could only get better from here.

"Thanks," Polly said. "I just wish I had a good place to wear it. I don't get out much." Part of the revolving clothes rack extended along the right wall of the store, outside of Polly's view. The plastic stirred, and to Melinda's horror, a leather jacket slid free.

"Really?" Jack said, apparently gathering his courage. "There's a—a dance. At the Veteran's Hall. On Friday. Maybe you and I could—"

The jacket glided toward Polly's back, empty arms outstretched. Jack saw it and the words died in the air before him. Melinda dashed up behind Polly and snatched at the jacket. It wriggled and struggled, the dry leather sliding through her hands.

"Stop it!" she hissed at the empty air. "Leave him alone!"

Polly spun in surprise and stared at Melinda. Melinda clutched at the jacket, trying to hold it still. It twisted and squirmed, as indignant as a child. Melinda forced a smile to her face and yanked the jacket closer to her body.

"Just bringing this in," she said. "It's all stiff and dirty. Can't do a thing with it."

Polly continued to stare. "Oh. Sure."

"Um, Friday?" Jack said hurriedly. "I was thinking before the dance, we could get a bite to—"

The jacket leaped from Melinda's grasp and shot up to the ceiling. It slapped the tiles with the sound of dry bones, then slammed back down to the floor. Polly's mouth fell open.

"Now how did I do that?" Melinda said with a patently fake little laugh. "I swear, I can trip over a smooth floor."

The jacket's sleeves reached up, a caricature of a baby reaching for its mother. Polly clutched her dress and fled the store, trailing a scream. The customer bell jingled merrily as the door slammed behind her.

Cold breath washed over Melinda's neck and a voice whispered, *"Underneath."* Fear trickled over Melinda's skin, a combination of fear and longing, and neither emotion was her own. She felt them nonetheless. The fear was thin and shrill, tinged with unfairness, a cook locked out of her own kitchen while a stranger lit it on fire. The longing ran deep and familiar, like a child looking for a lost blanket. Melinda turned, hoping to get a glimpse of the spirit who felt this way. Nothing behind her but empty air.

"Dammit!" Jack hurried around the counter, intending to go after Polly. He tripped over something Melinda couldn't see, stumbled, caught his balance, and gave up. "Shit!"

Melinda picked up the jacket and laid it on the counter. It lay motionless. "I'm sorry," she said.

"*You're* sorry?" he snapped. "My customers are being driven away, I'm barely staying afloat, and the one time my mouth actually works around Polly Whitehall, this . . . *thing* shows up and scares her away. I thought you were supposed to *help*."

Anger rose, and a retort popped into Melinda's mouth. She wanted to snarl that she wasn't causing Jack's problems, that she didn't get anything out of helping spirits cross over. It wasn't as if Jack were paying her. She was doing him a favor, for heaven's sake. But she took one look at his pained, angry face and swallowed the retort.

Most living people will get angry when you try to tell them a spirit is hanging about, Grandma always said. They get angry because they don't want to believe you or because they feel guilty about something or because telling them rakes up painful memories. Just remember that they aren't angry at you, and yelling back at them never helps. It might make you feel better for a few minutes, but it won't help the spirit cross over, and it won't help the living deal with their pain.

Jack wasn't angry at her. He was angry at the ghost who was haunting his shop. He was angry at the situation. And he was angry at himself for not asking Polly out sooner. Melinda was just the closest target for all of it.

"I'm sorry," she said again. "I know it's hard."

"You bet it's hard," he said. "I have a business loan and bills to pay and a father who's just waiting for me to fail so he can say 'I told you so.' Please, I just want to be alone, okay?"

Melinda nodded and left the store.

Sunlight washed over her as she stepped onto the sidewalk. Downtown Grandview stretched out before her, drowsing beneath a blue afternoon sky. Melinda took a moment to orient herself, as she often had to do after dealing with the dead. The big square ahead of her boasted its coppery green statue of two soldiers, and cars buzzed lazily around it. Small shops and little restaurants lined the streets, and the smells of Italian cooking, coffee, and fresh bread helped ground Melinda in the world of the living. Even a small brush with a spirit left her a little unsettled. Her usual remedy was coffee, and she decided this would be the perfect excuse for a double latte. And maybe a bagel. With raisins. And strawberry cream cheese.

A few moments later, she elbowed open the door to Same As It Never Was, her own antique shop. Two lidded Styrofoam cups from Village Java made a fragrant tower under her chin, and the Au Pair box of bagels weighed down her free hand. The customer bell rang, a more friendly echo to the one in Jack's Dry Cleaning shop. Andrea Morena looked up from her position behind the counter. She was a pretty, dark-skinned woman with a ready smile and strong, wiry hands.

"Ooooo! The Au Pair special," Andrea said. "Since Jim is nowhere in sight, can I assume that you intend to spoil my diet instead of his dinner?"

"I don't allow my business partners to diet," Melinda said. "It makes them cranky. Here."

Melinda carefully deposited her loot on the countertop. Smells of coffee and creamy strawberries leaked through paper and Styrofoam to permeate the shop. Sunlight slanted through the front display windows and bounced off the pale walls, giving the place a bright, airy feel. Antiques of all kinds waited patiently on shelves, on the floor, and in display cases arranged with a unique twist that truly defined the store. Dolls, vintage clothing, musical instruments, small pieces of furniture, ceramic figurines, records, toys, a collection of presidential campaign buttons from the thirties—all of them offered themselves for sale to any customer who cared to look. Melinda had decided long ago that her shop would never have the cramped, dusty feel that seemed to be the standard condition at other antique stores. Melinda didn't enjoy getting grit and dust on her hands, and she didn't particularly like stumbling around dimly lit shops with narrow aisles and squeaky floors. And if *she* didn't like it, why would her customers? Besides the eye-catching arrangements, Melinda insisted on breathing space, even if it meant keeping less merchandise on display.

The strategy seemed to work. Same As It Never Was did a thriving business. The only regret Melinda had these days was in the store's name. It had seemed like a good idea at the time, but she hadn't realized how annoying it would be for customers to write it on checks or how often they would ask, "Can I just write 'SAINW'?"

Melinda unstacked the coffee cups, handed one to Andrea across the counter, and opened the packet of bagels. At the moment, the shop was empty, and Andrea seemed to be going over an inventory spreadsheet on a laptop computer.

"You just missed a major rush," Andrea said. "Nine LOLITS, and four of them doll collectors. The other five had more eclectic tastes. I'm getting it all entered into the computer just now."

"Little Old Ladies in Tennis Shoes," Melinda said, sipping coffee. "My favorite kind of customer."

"That's because you didn't have to listen to their stories," Andrea groused. She reached for one of the bagel halves. Strawberry cream cheese made a fluffy pink cloud atop it.

"I *like* their stories," Melinda protested. "They're antiques, too, you know, and fun to hear."

"Not when they're just thin excuses to convince me why I should lower the price," Andrea growled. She pulled her straight black hair into a fake bun and pitched her voice like a sweet old woman's. " 'My dear Gerrold and I used to vacation here together, and it was so lovely. The ice cream parlor is gone, but the statue out there hasn't changed a bit. Gerrold's passed away now, and I'm on a fixed income these days. It's so difficult.' " Andrea's voice abruptly hardened. "'Do you think I could have this for ten dollars instead of twenty?' "

Melinda laughed, a little too long. "Thanks. I needed that."

"Glad to oblige, but what's wrong? Tough ghost?"

"Like phantom jerky."

Andrea nodded. She knew about Melinda's gift, her ability to see and talk to spirits and help them cross over. Melinda had been hesitant about telling her, but had finally taken the plunge. To Melinda's surprise, Andrea had been levelheaded and accepting of the whole thing. As a bonus, Melinda found it was a tremendous relief to have someone besides Jim to confide in. Jim Clancy was the best husband imaginable, but sometimes Melinda just wanted to talk to another woman. Besides, with Andrea in the know, Melinda didn't have to come up with fake explanations if she had to leave the store at odd moments. The dead didn't respect business hours.

"The ghost at Jack's Dry Cleaning?" Andrea gave her a sympathetic smile.

Melinda leaned on the counter and recounted the incident between bites of bagel and sips of coffee. "I've gone over there three times and I'm still stumped," she admitted. "Mostly because I have nothing to go on."

"Have you done any research?"

"Of course! Jack says no one close to him has ever died. He has no enemies, living or dead. He only moved to Grandview a few weeks ago. There seems to be no reason for a ghost to be following him around."

"What about the store?"

Melinda paused mid-munch. "The store?"

"The dry cleaning store. What if the ghost isn't connected to Jack? What if it's connected to his store?"

"I'd thought of that," Melinda said. "But I don't know anything about the building, and I didn't get a chance to look into it. Every time I talked to Jack, clothes tried to wrap us up. Do you know anything about it?"

"The place was empty when I first moved to Grandview," Andrea said, reaching for the computer. "But I'm relatively new to the area. Let's see if there's anything online about it."

The customer bell rang and both women looked up. A man entered the shop. He looked to be in his late thirties and was tall, nearly six feet, with a broad build, square face, and red hair the color of an autumn leaf. He wore a green-checked flannel shirt, jeans, and brown work boots. His blue eyes were hesitant, and he carried a file folder in large hands.

"Not buying," Melinda murmured to Andrea. "Wants to sell. I'm guessing estate sale."

"Unsure manner, file folder probably full of photos, work clothes from clearing out someone else's house," Andrea agreed quietly. "Cute, though. We in the market for more stuff?"

"Depends." Melinda turned toward him and smiled. "Hi! Can I help you?"

The man straightened and put on a friendly smile that creased his face and made him even better-looking. Melinda was forced to admit he could give Jim a run for his money. He put out his hand and Melinda shook it. Warm, dry, and firm.

"Kevin Ray," he said. "Are you the owner?"

"That's me," she said. "Melinda Gordon. This is Andrea Morena, my partner."

Kevin greeted Andrea and set the folder on the counter. Melinda automatically scanned the area around him, looking for ghosts. She didn't see any, which was a relief. It was a lot easier to deal with living strangers when the dead weren't vying for her attention at the same time.

"My great-grandmother Florence died recently," Kevin said.

"I'm sorry to hear that," Melinda said.

"Thanks," Kevin said. "But she had a long life. She was a hundred and one years old and lived in the same house her entire life."

"A hundred and one," Andrea said. "Wow! What was her secret? Cigars? Yogurt? Yoga?"

"I'm hoping it's good genes," Kevin said, slapping his own chest. "She was an interesting woman, but she rarely left her house. It's that big one out on Ray Road."

Something clicked in Melinda's head. "Ray! I didn't make the connection. I know that house. The huge Victorian place. The one that's . . . that's . . ." She trailed off and flushed a little.

"Falling apart?" Kevin finished for her. "Yeah, I know. Grandma Florence lived in a couple rooms on the first floor by herself. She refused to sell the place and no one else in the family wanted it, but she left it to me in her will. My wife and I want to restore it and turn it into a bed-and-breakfast."

"Now, that's something Grandview could use," Melinda said with a nod. The Chamber of Commerce, whose meetings Melinda attended regularly, worked hard to discourage chain restaurants and hotels. The plus side was that Grandview kept a thriving downtown, unspoiled by strip malls, Wal-Marts, and Super 8 Motels. The minus side was a lack of places for out-of-towners to stay. A new B&B would only be a good thing.

"That's what Sally and I think." Kevin opened the folder, revealing a pile of color photographs. "But restoring a house and putting together a B&B takes capital. Sally and I were wondering . . ." Now Kevin trailed off and gave Melinda a hopeful look that made him look like an Irish setter puppy.

". . . if any of Grandma Florence's old things might be worth selling on consignment," Andrea finished.

"Yeah. We want to keep some of the furniture, but a lot of it looks more valuable than comfortable. And she squirreled away a lot of interesting smaller stuff, some of it from the early 1900s. I brought some pictures."

Melinda turned to the photos. Pictures of furniture were on top of the stack. A pale oak blanket chest, lightly scarred but otherwise in fine condition. A lady's vanity with spindly legs and a fly-specked mirror. A squat oak dresser with brass handles on the drawers. A roll-top desk with four drawers and a matching chair upholstered with black leather. All of it looked solidly built and at least a century old. Melinda stared at them. She loved antiques. Ever since she was a little girl, old objects had seemed to call to her. They were heavy with history, filled with silent stories. These were objects that had been used by people with loves and fears and desires. The people were gone, their stories faded, but these objects remained behind, silent witnesses to entire lifetimes, and they fascinated Melinda to no end.

The businesswoman in her finally gave the rest of her a mental kick.

"These are some beautiful pieces," she said. "This desk is especially fine. I should warn you that I'm a little crowded right now. If you can store these pieces, I think you have several that a few of my customers have been looking for. I can act as a go-between. To be honest, you might be better off trying eBay. Their commission will be lower, for one thing."

"Nuh-uh!" Kevin said, putting up his hands. "Crating and shipping this stuff? What a nightmare!"

"That's my attitude," Melinda said with a light laugh. "Andrea's been after me to get a website going, but mail order . . . not how I want to spend my days."

"I've told you I'll handle all that," Andrea protested. "It wouldn't be—"

"Lay-ter," Melinda sang, then turned to Kevin. "Old argument, new audience. Anyway, I can probably sell the furniture for you, but we'd have to keep it at the house until it sold because I don't have the storage space. Would that work for you?"

"No problem," Kevin said. "What about the other stuff? These are just samples—there's lots more."

"Let's see." Melinda flipped through more photographs. Andrea bent her head to look, as well. A set of silver-backed hairbrushes and matching combs, tarnished but in excellent condition. Cast-iron hand tools were laid out beside a hand-carved toolbox. A kerosene lamp with a dusty chimney. A wooden cribbage board, also hand-carved. Melinda stared at the photos. The pieces were all in excellent condition and easily salable. She doubted they'd stay on her shelves for more than a few days. The cribbage board she wanted for herself, though she knew she should leave it in the shop. Jim would protest—rightly—that she didn't even play cribbage and wouldn't learn, no matter how good her intentions. That didn't stop her from wanting the board in a bad way.

"What's that thing?" Andrea asked, pointing to one photo. "It looks like some binoculars lost a fight with a slide rule."

"That's a stereoscope," Melinda said. "Remember those plastic View-Masters? You put that white cardboard disk into it, pushed the lever, and you could see different pictures?"

"Oh yeah," Andrea said. "My brother had one of those. He wouldn't let me look. He said the pictures were too scary. I looked anyway when he wasn't around, and it was just shots of Disney movies and stuff."

"This is the Victorian version," Melinda said.

"You looked at postcards with it and pretended you were there. Mr. Ray, these are some wonderful pieces. Are you sure you want to part with them?"

"What am I going to do with it all?" Kevin asked. "Open a museum? I'd rather it went to people who will appreciate it. When can you come out to see the rest?"

"How about early this evening? My husband is working until eleven, so it's not as if there's anything going on for me at home. I can look around and we can talk contracts and commissions."

"Can I come?" Andrea said. "I love poking around old houses."

"Oh, good—save me the effort of persuading you," Melinda said. "Six o'clock work, Mr. Ray? It'll still be light out."

"Kevin, please," he said. "And that'll be perfect."

As he turned to go, Andrea said, "Hey, can you tell me something?"

Kevin Ray turned back with a questioning look.

"You've lived in Grandview a long time, right?" Andrea said.

"I left for a few years to get my degree," Kevin said. "But other than that, yeah. Why?"

"Can you tell me what used to be in the store that's now Jack's Dry Cleaning?"

"The Mazurek Bakery," Kevin replied promptly. "But Dina Mazurek died—stroke, or something—

and the place died with her. Jack Perry took it over after that. I hear he's not doing too well. A shame."

"Maybe things'll pick up for him," Melinda said with a smile. "Thanks! See you this evening."

He left, and Melinda turned to Andrea. "Nicely done, Ms. Moreno."

"Thank you, Ms. Gordon." Andrea took another bite of bagel. "Do I get a promotion?"

Melinda made an arcane gesture over Andrea's head. "I now pronounce you senior partner."

"What was I before?"

"Regular partner. Let me see that computer." She tapped a few keys, brought up a search engine, and tapped a few more. Text and images flickered to life. "Aha! Mazurek isn't a very common name, and there's a Kaye Lynn Mazurek right here in Grandview."

Andrea leaned over to look. "Check for Dina's obituary. They usually list the names of surviving relatives."

"Way ahead of you." More key clicks. "Yep! Kaye Lynn's her daughter. Divorced, she went back to her maiden name . . . And there are some adult grandkids. The obituary doesn't mention the bakery except to say that Dina was the owner for many years. I think I'll have to stop over there again. Tomorrow, though. I've got enough going on tonight."

"Don't you mean *we*?" Andrea said archly.

"Right, right. In fact, if you don't mind, I'm going to pop over to the station and let Jim know about *our* trip to the Ray house." She headed for the door. "I don't want him to worry if he gets home before I do."

"It'd be way easier to call him," Andrea pointed out impishly.

"But not as much fun as dropping in on him," Melinda replied.

Andrea waved her off. "Newlyweds."

"You're just jealous."

"Insanely. Now go."

Outside, Melinda strode down the sidewalk toward the fire station. Jim Clancy, her husband of barely a year, was an EMT. He and his team were stationed at the local fire station, playing cards and waiting for calls they hoped would never come. How Jim put up with that kind of stress, she never knew. On the other hand, he didn't know how she put up with not knowing when a restless spirit would pop into her life and demand her help. In some ways they were a strange pair—he tried to stop living people from dying, and she tried to get dead people to accept that life was over. But she wouldn't have it any other way. Even now she noticed her footsteps quicken at the thought of seeing him, even if it was only to tell him her plans for the evening.

She passed Village Java, but the coffee smells were no longer enticing now that she'd had her caffeine fix. Up ahead, Jack's Dry Cleaning seemed to be closed. Through the window, she could see two people inside. Curious, Melinda drew closer. As she reached out to touch the door, the glass shattered.

2

MELINDA LEAPED BACK with a yelp. Then she recovered herself and tried to open the door. It was locked. Quickly, she ducked through the jagged opening left by the broken glass in the door's lower half. Chaos had erupted inside the store. Shirts, trousers, and dresses whipped through the air. Hangers jittered on rods like chattering teeth. A fountain of receipt paper spouted from the cash register. Jack Perry huddled next to the counter, his arms wrapped around his head. In the center of the store, untouched by the swirling chaos, stood a woman in her early thirties. She wore a severe suit of gray wool with a knee-length skirt, a high-necked blouse of white silk, and no-nonsense, black lace-up shoes. Her brown hair was rammed into a tight bun secured by a series of thin pins. Hard gray eyes surveyed the store, seeking, searching. She had a long nose, a square chin, and even, plain features. Her gaze alighted on Melinda, and for a moment Melinda thought the woman must be the shop's ghost, but only for a moment. She could see that this woman was very much alive.

A chill slid down Melinda's spine and she felt another pair of eyes, cold and hard, staring at her from behind. She spun around. A ghost stood there. She was white-faced, with short gray hair and sunken eyes. Her lips were as red as the writing on a birthday cake. Flour streaked her hair and puffed from her full-length apron. It had to be Dina Mazurek. Her expression was frantic, and a wave of fear thundered over Melinda. Melinda's heart pounded at the back of her throat and her hands shook like ice cubes jigging in a glass. Dina pointed toward the counter.

"Stop her!" Dina howled. *"Underneath!"*

She vanished. Melinda's fear evaporated along with her, and she staggered a little under the sudden shift of emotion. Sharing the feelings of the dead was an occasional side effect of her talent. Usually she could keep it under control, but Dina's fear had been so strong, it had made Melinda want to flee the shop.

Melinda turned back to face the rest of the store. When Dina had disappeared, the dancing clothes had dropped to the floor. The hangers went still. The mass of cash register paper floated to the counter. The strange woman in gray regarded it all with impersonal slate-gray eyes while Jack uncurled himself and walked unsteadily over to her.

"That was the worst it's ever gotten," he said. "What happened?"

"Your visitor is angry and frightened," the woman said. "But that doesn't matter—the visitor has no business being here. Fortunately, Mr. Perry, I've seen exactly this sort of thing many times before and the situation is easily within my ability to handle. Here's my card." She handed Jack a bit of pasteboard. "Call me and we'll set up an appointment."

With that, she strode with firm steps toward the door. Melinda found herself stepping aside for her as if for a duchess. The woman gave Melinda a small nod, opened the door—it was now unlocked—and left. Who the hell was she?

As she exited, Melinda felt something else brush by. Surprised, Melinda ducked outside in time to see the woman moving toward a car parked at the curb. The hazy figure of a man hovered behind her as she unlocked and got in. Melinda couldn't make out the ghost's features very well, though she got the impression that he was quite a lot older than the woman. He seemed to sense Melinda looking at him, because he glanced in her direction and vanished. Melinda watched the woman pull smoothly away into traffic.

The entire encounter with Dina and the gray woman had lasted less than three minutes, but it left Melinda completely mystified. Who was the woman? Did she have the same ability Melinda did? If she did, why did she seem completely unaware that a spirit was following her? And what was her connection to Jack Perry?

Easy enough to find out the answer to the last question, she decided, and went back into the store. Jack was picking up clothes with the resigned air of someone who had performed a particular chore too many times to count and knew he'd probably have to do it again.

"What was that all about?" Melinda asked without preamble.

"She's going to help me," Jack said, sliding a pair of green gabardine slacks back onto their hanger.

"Jack, I've only been working on this for a week." Melinda realized she was sounding defensive but couldn't stop herself. "Sometimes these things take time."

"I don't have time!" Jack moaned. "My business is dying and I'm going to be out on the street. I need to get rid of this . . . this *thing*—now. She wants to try, and I'm going to let her."

Melinda sighed and bent down to pick up a pink blouse, but Jack caught her wrist.

"Look, I appreciate your help," he said. "But I'm . . . gonna let her try."

Melinda shrugged and handed him the blouse. "It's your store," she said. "If you need me—"

"Okay."

"Okay." But as she passed the counter, Melinda caught sight of the woman's card lying on it. Jack was straightening a long skirt, so Melinda gave the card a quick look.

WENDY KING
SPIRITUAL CONSULTANT

The card listed a phone number but no address. The name meant nothing to Melinda. And what on Earth was a spiritual consultant? It sounded like a title used by a minister who didn't want to admit to being a minister. Or like something Melinda did. Was that why she had a ghost attached to her?

Lost in thought, Melinda left Jack's store and trotted over to the fire station to find Jim. She found him chatting with one of the firefighters as he leaned against the rear doors of "his" ambulance, which was parked alongside the station. Melinda felt her heart flip, and she found herself smiling. No doubt about it, she had married a handsome man. Dark brown hair that framed his face in soft waves. Intense blue eyes. Strong jaw, thin lips, feathery eyebrows. A killer build. A bit of warmth flowed over her at the sight of him, and she wanted to feel his arms around her, his hands on her skin, his lips over hers. This was her husband, and would be for the rest of her life. For a moment she wondered what it would be like to be married to him when they were both old and gray, with wrinkles and gnarled joints. Would she feel the same little jolt every time she saw him? Melinda's parents had split up when she was a child and neither she nor her mother had seen Melinda's father in over fifteen years, so she couldn't ask her mother if she felt it, and it hadn't been something she'd ever asked her grandmother. Grandma had died long before Melinda had first laid eyes on Jim. Grandma would have liked Jim, and it was one of Melinda's bigger regrets that they'd never have the chance to meet. Well, the only way to find out if the little jolt would still be there after thirty, forty, and fifty years would be to hang around long enough to find out. The thought was a pleasant prospect.

Jim's eye fell on Melinda as she approached and a quizzical look crossed his face. She leaned toward him in a silent request for a kiss and got one. He smelled of hospital soap, a familiar Jim smell. The firefighter he'd been talking to sketched a quick wave and vanished into the fire station.

"You didn't abandon Andrea at the store just to get one of those from me?" Jim said with a quiet smile.

"Have to," she said, "until you find a way to send them FedEx."

"Uh-huh. What's going on?"

"Got a date tonight—me, Andrea, and a house-ful of antiques. Potential estate sale. I'll be out late and just wanted you to know in case you beat me home."

His expression became wary and he crossed his arms. His blue EMT uniform gave him a serious air. "Is this a ghost thing?"

"Haven't seen any so far," she said, then narrowed her eyes. "And so what if there are ghosts? What does it matter?"

"It matters because I need to know how much worrying I have to do. You're already stressed out about Jack Perry's place."

"Ah. In that case—absolutely no ghosts," she reassured him. "It'll be a big sale, major boost for the store. It's the Ray place. Kevin Ray is fixing it up and turning it into a B-and-B. You might want to drop by, exchange manly renovation tips with him."

Jim and Melinda's "new" house was a fixer-upper they'd gotten for half a song because it needed extensive renovations. In theory, the two of them worked on the house together, but in practice Jim did most of the work. Melinda helped wherever and whenever she could.

Melinda got another kiss from Jim and returned to the store, eyeing the broken glass on Jack's Dry Cleaning as she went. No sign of the woman or of Dina's ghost. Inside, Jack swept shards, his face set. Melinda's heart went out to him. He was trying so hard, and he didn't know what to do, but she couldn't force him to accept her help. Maybe Wendy King, whoever she was, could help him where Melinda couldn't. If that were the case, more power to her. The important thing was that Dina crossed over and left Jack to his shop. Still, the raw fear Dina had felt made Melinda uneasy.

That evening at the antique shop, Andrea flipped the door sign to CLOSED while Melinda gathered up her keys. They got into Melinda's red Saturn SUV and drove toward the outskirts of town. The sun was still high, though clouds were slipping in from the west, promising an early twilight.

"Ray family, Ray Street," Andrea commented as Melinda turned right. "Sounds like they've been in Grandview for a while."

"Long enough to collect some interesting antiques," Melinda said. "This'll be more fun than Christmas."

Ray Street headed west out of town, where the number of houses dwindled. About half a mile down the road they came to the Ray house. Melinda had seen it before, of course—had driven past it numerous times—but she had never really looked at it closely. The house was a generous three-story Queen Anne mansion, "stick style," if Melinda was any judge. Everything was straight up and down. Three towers pushed their spindly fingers toward the sky. The roof over the front porch was supported by a series of thin pillars, and spiky posts made up a railing both on the floor of the porch and on several balconies above. Tall shutters flanked the narrow windows, several of which were boarded up. The roofline made a series of irregular points, each topped with a lightning rod or weather vane. The house itself had once been painted a deep red, with a slightly darker red for the trim, but the paint had faded and peeled, leaving the house looking dull and scabby. The grounds were overgrown—knee-high grass, looming bushes, flower beds lost among weeds and vines. A low wrought-iron fence drew a strict boundary around the yard, with a wide gap for the driveway. Melinda carefully guided the SUV onto the cracked cement and parked in front of a leaning carriage house that had been converted into a garage at some point.

"Wow," Andrea said. "All you need is a set of tombstones in the front yard and *poof!* Instant haunted house."

"Don't even," Melinda said. "I'm hoping to get through this ghost-free for once."

"Yeah, good luck with that." Andrea got out of the car. "I'm predicting you'll have to deal with at least three ghosts in this house before this is over."

Melinda slammed the SUV door. "Why do you keep saying stuff like that?"

"Murphy's law." At Melinda's blank look, she continued. "Listen, if I said, 'Goodness, no—we won't see any ghosts,' it would practically guarantee a whole bunch of spirits, right? So now I'm telling you we're going to see a whole gaggle of ghosts, and that means we won't see any at all."

"The problem with that logic," Melinda said, heading for the house, "is that you've jinxed it. You said there won't be ghosts because you said there will be, which means there *will* be ghosts, since you effectively said there *won't* be, right?"

"Ah, but then *you* double-jinxed it just now by saying there *will* be ghosts after all, which means there *won't* be." Andrea laughed. "And I think we'd better stop there because I left my spare brain back at the store."

They made their way up the front walk. Long ago, someone had planted daylilies alongside it as a border, and they had run wild, throwing their tendrils into the pathway like green tentacles. It was impossible for Melinda to pick her way through them without long leaves brushing against her calves and ankles.

The porch steps creaked, of course. Sawhorses, lumber, and various power tools were scattered about the porch itself, and a city builder's permit had been nailed to the front door, which meant someone was at least semi-serious about renovating the place. A sticky note stuck to the permit read:

MELINDA & ANDREA: DOORBELL'S BROKEN. COME IN AND SHOUT.

Melinda pushed the double front door open onto a generous foyer. A large staircase ahead of her wound toward the upper floors. The floors were sanded hardwood with the finish worn away beneath decades of traveling feet. Doorways opened left and right into large rooms filled with the indistinct white shapes of furniture covered with sheets. The place smelled of sawdust and autumn air—most of the first-floor windows were open, and a gentle breeze stirred the air.

"Hello?" Andrea called. "Kevin? We're here!"

Silence. Then footsteps thudded on the floor above and Kevin came down the turns of the main staircase. Sawdust salted his ruddy hair. "Is it six already? Lost track of time. Come in! I'll give you the dollar tour and show you some of the stuff we're trying to sell."

He took them through the sprawling first floor—a parlor, a sitting room, a dining room, a kitchen, and a drawing room. Sunlight slanted in through tall, narrow windows. Threadbare carpets did little to muffle their echoing footsteps, and covered furniture stood everywhere. Out of habit, Melinda kept a sharp eye out for ghosts, but saw nothing out of the ordinary and finally let herself relax. Kevin pulled several of the dust covers aside to show Melinda and Andrea what he had. Andrea took pictures with a digital camera and Melinda took copious notes. He showed them antique tables, dining room chairs, love seats, and settees. Once he whipped away a sheet to reveal a clavier, an old console-style piano complete with brass candleholders on movable arms that could be swung closer to the music. Tiny droplets of wax still stuck to the ivory keys. The cabinet was of solid walnut. Melinda made a small sound of pleasure, touched a few notes. The sounds were clear, if out of tune.

"I know just the buyer for this," Melinda said. "He'll go crazy."

"You mean Ned Zhang," Andrea agreed, and turned to Kevin. "He collects old musical instruments, and he's been looking for a high-quality clavier for ages. You'll have to beat him away with a wrecking ball when he hears about this."

"Music to my ears," Kevin said with a grin.

The kitchen was filled with well-used appliances from the sixties that seemed to be still in use. The ancient tile floor had been recently scrubbed but still bore the scars of decades of dirt. A small table surrounded by benches sat in the breakfast nook, and the faint smell of coffee hung in the air.

"Anything in here you want to part with?" Melinda asked. "I don't think much of it will be worth anything."

"No, not really," Kevin said. "This was the only

part of the house Grandma Florence was using before she died. She kept a cot in that corner and used the bathroom down the hall. We tried to get her to leave, but she absolutely refused. Her mind was still sharp, and there was no way to force her to move into a nursing home or assisted living. Anyway, my wife and daughter and I are sort of living here and sort of living in our own place while we're doing the renovations. We're eventually going to knock this wall out and expand the kitchen, make it meet commercial standards. Until then, Grandma Florence's old appliances will do for us."

Melinda found she'd been bracing herself for the icy chill of a spirit, but felt nothing. "How long did she live here by herself?"

"Decades." Kevin leaned against a tiled counter, his plaid work shirt rolled up past well-muscled forearms. "She had three sons, but she outlived them all, and her grandchildren are scattered. My mom—her granddaughter—was the only one of her descendants who really gave a damn about her or this place. Mom brought me and my sister out here all the time when we were little. When I grew up, I visited when I could, but you know how it goes. Whenever I asked if she was lonely, Grandma Florence said she was perfectly fine. I think she liked the fact that she was still living completely on her own at her age, to tell the truth. I tried to hire someone to mow the lawn for her and such, but she wouldn't hear of it. 'Let it go,' she said. 'I never go outside to see it, so what's it matter?' "

"She never went outside?" Andrea said.

"Almost never," Kevin said. "She wasn't afraid to. She just . . . didn't." His gaze went somewhere else for a moment. "I miss her more than I thought I would. Wicked sense of humor. When she told a joke, you laughed until your stomach hurt." He shook his head and reached for the refrigerator handle. "Sorry—where are my manners? Would you like a bottle of water? It's thirsty work tromping around this place."

Both women accepted. Bottles in hand, they trooped upstairs, where Kevin showed them more furniture and trunkloads of smaller antiques, several of which took Melinda's breath away.

"These are wonderful," she said, carefully fingering an ivory-handled straight razor. Carved ivy leaves twined up the handle. Next to it on the dresser was a hand-painted porcelain washbowl and pitcher, a man's ivory comb, and a glass bottle of hair pomade from the twenties. The latter was tightly capped and more than half full. "Kevin, seriously—these will move quickly, and we'll both make a tidy profit."

"Come down here," he said, heading for the door. "Got plenty more in the rooms at the other end of the hall."

The main hallway on the second floor had a

creaky wooden floor carpeted with a long woolen runner that had seen better decades. Its upper walls were of yellow plaster that met dark walnut wainscoting halfway down. The sunlight that had been coming in at the ends of the hallway was now growing dim. Melinda automatically flipped an ancient light switch, but nothing happened.

"Sorry," Kevin said. "Electricity up here doesn't work yet. It's on my list. But the windows in the bedroom down there face west and there's plenty of light yet." He headed for the main stairs, clearly intending to go up to the third floor.

"Wait." Andrea pointed down the corridor. "Isn't the bedroom down that way?"

Kevin paused, then turned, a sheepish look on his face. "Yeah. It is. We . . . we always go this way. Up to the third floor and down the back stairs when we want to get to that part of the house."

"Oh? How come?" Melinda asked.

"We've . . . that is . . . we've always done it. Ever since I was a kid. No one goes down that part of the hallway. Ever."

"Never?" Andrea asked, a little incredulously.

"Well, every once in a while someone would," Kevin admitted. "A guest in the house who didn't know, or someone who had to sweep the rug, I guess. But other than that—no. Never. My sister and I used to dare each other to run down it. Then we'd run away screaming. You know how kids are. Now I avoid it out of habit. That hallway is probably the main reason no one else in the family really wanted this house after Grandma Florence died."

Andrea shot Melinda a look that had *ghost* written all over it, but Melinda was already peering down the dim corridor, every sense she had on the lookout for something otherworldly. She didn't see a thing except the tired-looking blue runner on the floor.

"Is the hall scary or something?" Melinda asked.

Kevin leaned against the wall and took a swig from his water bottle. He glanced down the hallway, then looked away. "I don't know. Look, I never saw anything. I couldn't have."

"You seem awfully nervous for someone who never saw anything," Andrea said in that open, friendly way of hers. Coming from anyone else, the remark would have sounded offensive or accusatory, but coming from Andrea it was an invitation to talk.

"Ah, kid stuff. When you're eight, you'll believe anything." Kevin glanced down the hallway again. "Hell, it was nothing. One time when we were visiting at Thanksgiving, I came up here by myself while everyone else was downstairs finishing their pumpkin pie. The dining room was bright and hot and stuffy, but up here it was cool and dark. It was nice to get away. I walked down this same hallway. It had the same blue runner on the floor. I remember the wainscoting was at eye level for me back then, and I ran my finger along the top of it, and it was dusty. I could hear my family talking far below, and I decided to see what the big deal was with the back part of this hallway. No one ever *said* you couldn't go down there. You just didn't go. Everyone always went around.

"I went one step, then two, then ran back. Nothing happened. So I went three steps, and four. My heart was pounding hard enough to rattle my ears, but nothing happened. I kept going. I was feeling pretty brave by then, my steps getting more and more confident.

"I was a little more than halfway to the end. And then I saw a white thing lying on the hallway floor. It looked like a bit of mist. It seemed to glow a little in the darkness. I froze and stared at it. It was only three or four feet away, but when you're a kid and it's dark, that's a serious distance. I wanted to run, but I was also curious. Curiosity finally won out. I edged closer, then reached down to touch it."

"What happened?" Andrea whispered.

"It leaped up with a horrible flapping noise," Kevin said. "This great white thing lunged for me in the dark. I couldn't even scream. I just turned and ran. I knew it was reaching for me with cold fingers or claws. I ran and ran and that was when I heard it."

Melinda realized her mouth was hanging open and she closed it. "Heard what?"

"Jean—my sister—laughing. I had walked past her without seeing her because she was hiding around a turn on the main staircase, partway up to the third floor. She had a piece of Grandma Florence's black yarn in her hand. The other end was tied to a white pillowcase she had laid on the hallway floor. One good yank on the yarn, and the pillowcase flew upward at me."

"Oh, no!" Andrea said, half laughing herself. "You have an evil sister!"

"I got so mad at her." Kevin shook his head. "I chased her up the main stairs to the third floor, down the back stairs, and, without realizing it, back through this hallway. Jean was shrieking and laughing the whole time. Then she tripped and fell right at the spot where she'd put the pillowcase. I grabbed for her, and straight out of the floor came this ragged white hand. I could see through it. It grabbed for my legs. I screamed then. Jean managed to roll over. She saw it and screamed. The hand groped around, like it belonged to someone who was buried in the floor. Both of us ran then, ran all the way downstairs and outside to the front porch.

"Mom came out to see what all the noise was about, and we just told her we were playing. Jean and I never talked about it ever again, and we never went down that hallway, either. Silly stuff. Overactive imaginations of kids who'd had too much dessert."

Melinda suppressed an urge to purse her lips. Children were often able to see ghosts but lost the ability as they grew older. Melinda suspected it was because the adult mind, forced by a science-dominated society to become analytical, refused the existence of spirits so strongly that it affected perception. Only a handful of people retained their childhood ability to see spirits into adulthood, and not even all of them admitted to it. Melinda's own mother refused to believe in her own gift. A small, familiar pang touched Melinda's stomach at the thought, but she pushed the feeling aside. This wasn't the time to be thinking about that.

"But I notice you still won't go down that hallway," Melinda observed. "You said your whole family avoided it, too. How come?"

"Like I said, I'm not totally sure," Kevin said. "There's a family legend, and it's probably what got me and my sister all worked up. Grandma Florence had a brother named Arthur. He died in an accident decades ago, before even my parents were born. He's supposedly hanging around, doing weird stuff."

"You think it was Uncle Arthur's arm?" Andrea said, echoing Melinda's own thoughts.

"I think it was too much whipped cream on the pumpkin pie," Kevin said firmly, "and I think it's ridiculous that a grown man won't walk down a hallway in his own house. What am I going to do—tell my bed-and-breakfast guests they shouldn't go down there? Come on."

And he strode down the hall.

3

MELINDA AND ANDREA stared at Kevin's back as it faded into the gloom, then traded looks.

"Well?" Andrea whispered. "You're Ghost Girl. Aren't you going to follow?"

Melinda rolled her eyes and headed after him. Andrea brought up the rear. The hallway was very long, and Melinda noticed there were no doors on the right wall, though the left had two. Both were open. One led into an empty closet, the other into a dingy bathroom. The dark walnut wainscoting seemed to absorb what little dim light there was, and the dingy walls loomed over her. Floorboards creaked, and Melinda felt them shift beneath her weight. The air closed in, and her hands—one clutching the water bottle, the other her notepad—grew cold. Fear crept up her spine. As they walked, Melinda saw the shadows at the border of the wainscoting shift. A dark hand rose from the blackness and made long fingers along the wall, reaching, grasping toward Kevin. Melinda gasped. Andrea and Kevin both stopped.

"What's wrong?" Andrea asked.

The hand dropped back into the shadows. Melinda looked at the spot where it had been for a moment. "Nothing," she said. "It's dark, and I thought I saw something move. Where's that bedroom?"

"Almost there," Kevin said. "This hallway feels longer than it is."

He turned to go. Andrea gave Melinda a quizzical look. *Caused by a ghost?* Melinda shook her head, but when Andrea also turned, Melinda let her notebook drop quietly to the floor before she trotted ahead to catch up.

At the end of the hall, two doors faced each other. Kevin opened the one on the left and ushered Andrea and Melinda in. Orange light from the setting sun poured in through two windows. A canopied bed took up most of the floor space. A night stand with three drawers stood next to it, and Melinda noticed a generous wardrobe in the corner. The closet door was shut. Several china dolls were laid out on the bed, each with a tiny crinoline dress, faded ribbons, miniature black shoes. A crack ran across the face of one of them. It had red ribbons in its black hair.

"I'm not sure whose room this was," Kevin said.

"But there are a lot of clothes and toys in the closet. I put those dolls on the bed."

"They're nice," Andrea said, making a beeline for them. "And we just sold a bunch of these today, so our stock is low. Even the one with the crack should sell."

"Oh, shoot," Melinda said. "Dropped my notebook. I'll be right back." And she fled the room before either of them could say anything. She hurried back down the forbidden hallway and stopped where she had let her notebook fall.

"Hello?" she said quietly. "Are you here? I can see you. I can help you."

She listened hard and scanned the hall shadows. The yellowing plaster seemed to reach forward and backward, walling Melinda in with blank space. A little ahead of her, the closet and bathroom doors gaped like black pits. She smelled dry mold and old wood.

"Hello?" she said again. "Come on out—I saw you earlier. Let me help."

Nothing. Melinda listened a moment longer, then bent to retrieve her notebook with a sigh. She had seen a ghost, that much she knew, and so much for her hopes of getting through this estate sale ghost-free. Clearly this was one of the shy ones who would have to be coaxed out before she could help it cross over.

Melinda straightened and looked straight into an angry white face. The wide, pale eyes stretched and the mouth gaped and drooled. Wild hair squirmed and twisted. Two clawed hands reached for Melinda's neck with cold fingers. They trailed white cobwebs.

"Leave!" the mouth wailed. *"Run!"*

The strength drained from Melinda's knees. Every animal instinct shouted at her to run, but she couldn't. Fear rooted her feet, made them heavy. Like a bird watching an approaching snake, she stared into the ghost's oozing face.

"Go!" it screeched.

"I can help you," she whispered. Her dry tongue scraped the inside of her mouth. "I can—"

The ghost howled and swiped at Melinda's face. The hand passed through her with a soft, sick feeling, like a long, cold length of cotton batting being drawn out of her ears and nose. Nausea lumped in Melinda's stomach, and she flattened herself against the wall behind her. The ghost screamed and the plaster shook. The floor shuddered and the rug slid beneath her feet.

"Go!" the spirit screamed at her. *"Go!"*

Melinda fled. She sprinted down the hallway. Ahead of her lay the main staircase. She stopped and put a hand to her chest. Her heart pounded behind her rib cage and she was sweating the cold sweat of fear. Melinda glanced back down the hall-way. No sign of the ghost.

Melinda pulled the water bottle from her pocket and took a drink to settle herself, then climbed the stairs to the third floor, crossed the hallway that went above the ghost's hallway on the floor below, and took the back stairs down to the second floor. Her heart slowed, the sweat dried, and the analytical part of her mind set to work, pushing the fear aside and letting it drain away. The terror wasn't hers, it was the ghost's, and she could safely set it aside. It was a trick her mother had never mastered and it was, Melinda suspected, the main reason Mom continued to deny she even had the family gift. The trick helped keep Melinda from a nervous breakdown. Without it, she'd probably spend her days as a quivering puddle of protoplasm that flinched from shadows and waited for the next ghost to leap out at her.

The analytical side of her mind was definitely her most valuable tool, and right now it was telling her that she now knew why the Ray family avoided this particular section of the house. The spirit was territorial and angry. The question was, who was it and what did it want? In order to help it cross over, she needed to answer both those questions. She had gotten the impression the ghost was that of a young man, despite its appearance. Kevin had said Grandma Florence had a brother named Arthur, the one who had died in an accident decades ago. He was the most logical place to start.

In the bedroom, Melinda found Andrea carefully piling antique toys on the bed near the dolls. A wooden airplane, a tin fire engine, and a Noah's ark set, complete with little painted animals, made a little treasure trove on the ancient mattress. The closet door hung open and Kevin was watching Andrea. Neither of them showed any sign that they had heard anything strange from the hallway.

"Find it?" Kevin asked as she entered.

"Find what?" Melinda said, confused.

"Your notebook," he said. "That's why you left."

"Oh! Of course." Melinda held it up and managed a weak grin. "Right here. Looks like you have some more excellent pieces."

"Yeah, but the light's going," Andrea said. "I told Kevin we'll have to come back."

"Several times," Melinda said with a nod. "Listen, Kevin, cataloging everything is going to take days. It might be easier if you gave us permission to come and go, and we'll find you if we have questions or need to give you an update."

"Sounds perfect," Kevin said. "I'm in the middle of renovating the third-floor bathrooms, and I have a plumber coming in tomorrow afternoon and . . . anyway, yes—that would be fine."

"Then I'll draw up a consignment contract and bring it by tomorrow," Melinda said. "We can start selling some of this stuff right away."

"That sounds even more perfect," Kevin replied. "I have to pay the plumber."

Melinda waved away his offer to show them out, and a few minutes later, she and Andrea were driving back to Grandview.

"How many ghosts?" Andrea asked. "Don't deny it. I can tell."

"Just the one." Melinda sighed. "So much for double and triple jinxes."

"Was it that Uncle Arthur guy Kevin mentioned?"

"Maybe. I couldn't tell. He didn't want me hanging around." She shuddered. "Let's talk about something else."

"Okay. But I should probably tell you that I took a picture of the ghost." Andrea brandished the camera from her position in the passenger seat.

"You did?" Melinda asked, startled. "How? When did you see it?"

"When we were upstairs. I took a picture, but it came out too dark. So I asked the ghost to pose for another one, and it did."

"What?" Melinda started to turn and stare at her, then remembered she was driving and faced her eyes firmly forward again. "Are you serious?"

"I'm completely serious. I took another picture, but it *still* came out too dark. Then I realized what the problem was."

Melinda was completely baffled. "What?"

"The spirit was willing, but the flash was weak."

A long moment of silence followed. "You're fired," Melinda said.

Some time later, Melinda was sitting on the floor behind the coffee table in her living room. Jim sat beside her. White cardboard cartons made a miniature imperial city on the tabletop, and the smells of well-spiced takeout filled the living room. Sweet-and-sour pork, savory princess chicken, spring vegetables in mushroom sauce, tender fried rice, and crispy spring rolls all steamed in front of them. No plates. Melinda and Jim speared at the table, plucking food directly from the cartons with their chopsticks. Sauces dripped and gravy spattered. It was sloppy and messy and Melinda loved it.

"Why don't we do this more often?" Melinda asked, dropping a morsel of mushroom into her mouth.

"Because it's a royal pain to haul the coffee table into the yard and hose it off afterward," Jim said. "And you may as well get it over with."

"Over with?"

"Telling me about the ghost you ran into at the Ray place. It's written all over you."

Melinda held out an arm and pretended to examine it. "Where?"

"Right . . . here." Jim slid his finger up the crook of her elbow, sending a fine shiver all along Melinda's skin.

"You keep doing that and I won't say anything at all."

"Maybe I don't want you to."

"Then why did you ask?"

"Just being the sensitive husband." He leaned over and nibbled on her ear. More delicious shivers. "You smell like duck sauce. I like it."

Melinda couldn't help but laugh. "I'm still eating."

"Just making sure everything stays warm for later." Jim leaned back against the couch with half a spring roll. "So, tell me about the Ray place ghost. Get it off your chest."

Melinda did. "It's so frustrating," she finished. "I don't have much to go on. Between that one and the one haunting Jack Perry's shop, my batting average is pretty shot. Neither of them will talk to me, and Dina—she's Jack's ghost—just flings clothes around the shop and screams about something being underneath."

Jim cocked his head. "Do you ever get the urge to just yell at them? You know—'Quit being stupid and tell me what you want, dummy! I'm here to help!' "

"God, yes," Melinda said, rolling her eyes. "But only when I was younger. A friend of mine lived in an apartment building . . . I got involved with a ghost in the basement. I thought someone was calling me. But it was a ghost of an old woman crying. . . . She was so sad, so lost. 'Mittens! My mittens! I can't find my mittens!' God, I looked all over that basement for a pair of mittens. I looked in every corner, I pulled the pay washers and dryers away from the walls and looked behind them. I even tried to open the furnace. And the whole time this ghost kept saying, 'My mittens! You have to find my mittens!' She wouldn't help me look. She wouldn't tell me what they looked like. She wouldn't tell me where she last saw them.

"I was only about eighteen. This was one of the first times I'd tried handling a ghost without my grandmother's help, and I was *not* going to ask her. I was getting frustrated. The building super caught me down there looking once and threw me out because I wasn't a tenant, and I had to sneak back in the next day. When I did, the old woman's ghost popped up and started yelling at me. 'You need to find my mittens! Why can't you find my mittens, you stupid girl?' I got so angry at her, I yelled at her. I called her a bunch of names and told her she could find her own damn mittens. She started to scream. The lights flickered, and lids on the washers slammed up and down. I stomped out of the basement."

"What happened?" Jim asked.

Melinda shrugged. "The super heard all the noise and I got caught again. This time he hauled me into his apartment to call the police. He had like a million cats in there and it smelled awful. I finally persuaded him to call my grandmother instead of the police. She came and got me, but I was so upset. I was there to help, and instead I got myself in trouble."

"What did your grandmother say?"

"She took one look at the super's apartment, made me apologize to him, and took me outside to sit on the front steps. She pointed out that getting angry was making me miss the obvious."

Jim gave Melinda a quizzical look. "The obvious what?"

"Solution." Melinda plucked a bit of shrimp and ate it. "Grandma was smart. She let a few days pass so the super could calm down, and then she took me back to his apartment. She asked where he got his cats from. Turned out a tenant in the building, an old woman, had died a few years ago, leaving her cat behind. The super knew the cat—she was always escaping from the old woman's apartment and hiding in the basement. The super didn't want to send the cat to an animal shelter, so he kept her himself. But she was pregnant and had kittens."

"And the cat's name was Mittens," Jim finished.

"Yep," Melinda said. "I should have figured that out the minute the super took me into his apartment, but I was so ticked off, I wasn't thinking. Anyway, Grandma 'accidentally' let Mittens escape. She ran into the basement like she always did, and I volunteered to go get her. Once I was able to show the old woman that Mittens was safe and had a good home, she crossed over. Taught me something about anger management."

"But why didn't the old woman just *tell* you she was looking for her cat?" Jim said. "I mean, she could have saved you both a lot of grief."

"Spirits don't always see the world the same way we do," Melinda told him. "I think sometimes the dead can only partially see the living, or they get so focused on one thing that it's all they can talk about." She idly trailed a bit of spring roll through a puddle of spicy mustard. "You've seen it at work, I'm sure. People who get into a bad accident and then obsess over some little detail?"

"Oh yeah," Jim said with a nod. "Just yesterday I helped this teenage girl who had totaled her truck and almost died, but the whole time I was on the scene, the only thing she would talk about was how this CD she had just bought was scratched. The accident was too big for her to wrap her head around, so she focused on the CD because she could handle that."

"Exactly. I think the trauma of death does the same thing to a lot of ghosts. Whatever it is that keeps them from crossing over becomes an obsession. To a spirit, nothing exists except that one thing that keeps it here, just like to that girl, nothing existed except her CD. A lot of times, I *do* get angry with them, but there's really no point in showing it. You might as well get angry at a rock for being hard or at a man for liking big—"

"I think," Jim interrupted, "that you probably shouldn't finish that sentence. My revenge on behalf of males worldwide would have to be terrible."

"Yeah? What do you think you could do to me?"

"I'll eat all the Chunky Monkey ice cream by myself."

Melinda shrank away. "I'll be good."

"Speaking of which," Jim said, scrambling to his feet, "care to join me in a bowl?"

"Do you think we'll both fit?"

Melinda checked the address and parked. The Mazurek family lived in a smallish red-brick house tucked away down a tree-lined street only a few blocks from downtown Grandview. Melinda could have walked it from the antique store. If Dina had originally lived here, she had probably walked to her bakery. Melinda tried to imagine Dina

Mazurek, alive and well, stepping smartly through the street of Grandview to her own business, unlocking the front door and releasing the smells of yeast, flour, and sugar into the street, working in her large commercial kitchen, chatting and laughing with her workers, going over the books in her office. But now she was dead, and her spirit was so obsessed with something beneath, she couldn't cross over into the peace that was her birthright. Melinda hated approaching total strangers, but she couldn't just stand by and let a spirit's pain and torture continue. So she climbed down from the SUV and forced herself to stride up the walk to the Mazureks' front door.

The woman who answered Melinda's ring was a pleasant-faced woman with a fine-boned build. She had long, curly brown hair, gray eyes, a long nose, and a wide smile. Her outfit consisted of simple jeans and a green T-shirt. "Yes?"

Melinda introduced herself. "I'm looking for the Mazurek family. Is this the right house?"

"Yes," the woman said, a little guardedly.

"Oh, good. I run the antique store Same As It Never Was, right off the square?" Melinda gave her a smile and her card. "I'm thinking about starting a sort of newsletter about the history of Grandview—you know, history, antiques, they go together. Anyway, I heard that a woman named Dina Mazurek used to run a bakery downtown, and I was hoping to get some information about her and her business for the newsletter. Would you be able to help with that? I'd really appreciate it if you could."

"Dina was my mother," the woman said. "My name is Kaye Lynn. Why don't you come in?"

A few minutes later, the two women were sitting at Kaye Lynn's kitchen table. The kitchen was painted a bright, sunny yellow, and the sparkling windows let in plenty of autumn sunlight. Canisters and appliances neatly lined the cupboard. The dark wood table was a little battered, obviously used for serving up thousands of family meals. Currently, it was covered with three-by-five cards. An open textbook lay faceup on the table beside a ball of string, a tape dispenser, a set of markers, a pair of scissors, and two flyswatters with price tags still on them.

"I hope you don't mind that I keep working while we talk," Kaye Lynn said. "I have to get this done in time for school on Monday, and this is the only chance I'll have this weekend."

"What is it?" Melinda asked.

"Das Fliegenklatschespiel," she replied, picking up a card. "The flyswatter game. You tape vocabulary words to the board and give a flyswatter to two students, then give them a clue to the word. Whoever swats the word first wins. We're reviewing for a test." She wrote *das Brot* on a card, cut

a piece of string, and taped the string to the card. "My German I class is doing food right now. This is the word for bread."

"Sounds like fun," Melinda said.

Kaye Lynn smiled and reached for another card. "You'd think. Some kids really get into it, others lose on purpose so they can get out of participating. They act as if they'd rather do another worksheet. But you wanted to know about my mother."

Melinda took the cue. "She ran a bakery in town, is that right?"

"From before I was born until the day she died. Baking was her life. She loved everything about it, and she was so good at it. Some of her customers drove fifty, sixty miles to get her birthday cakes. 'We can't have a birthday without a Dina Mazurek cake,' they'd say." Kaye Lynn's eyes were touched with pride. "She was famous, in her way."

"How did she start the bakery?"

"Mom came from Germany and she brought two things to America with her—her mother's recipes and her grandmother's silver. She loved to bake and she loved working independently, so starting a business was a natural step. Mom sold the silver to get the startup money." Kaye Lynn adopted a German accent. "'What was I going to do? There's no point in having table silver if you have nothing to eat, no?' And so she got to work with a little store and her mother's recipes. The Mazurek Bakery was almost instantly a success, but it was a little awkward sometimes when I was growing up. Bakers work nights, you know."

"They do?"

"Oh, yes. How do you think those doughnuts and loaves of bread get on the shelves for early-morning customers? Mom kept a cradle for me in the bakery, and when I got older, she set aside my own play area. I slept there a lot while she worked."

"What about your father?"

"He traveled a lot with his job. And Mom kept as few employees as she could get away with. 'Why pay someone else to do what I can do myself?' she always said. So she had to work a lot. It meant that after school I'd go straight to the bakery and often spend the night there. I didn't mind, really. It smelled like home to me."

Melinda leaned her elbows on the table. "You didn't want to take over the business?"

"Not really," Kaye Lynn said with a shake of her head. "I'm a decent baker, but I don't really have the time or interest. Running a bakery would be my idea of hell." She gave a low laugh. Her voice was soft, but carried surprisingly well. "I suppose many people feel the same way about teaching teenagers. Mom was a little disappointed she wouldn't have anyone to hand her recipes down to, but she never pushed."

A little spark of excitement ignited within Melinda. "Her recipes?"

"Oh, yes. Mom kept her recipes a strict secret. That was one of the things that kept people coming back to the Kaye Lynn Bakery. No one knew exactly how Mom made her cakes and breads and cookies. She let the employees mix and bake, but she always added the ingredients personally. It was her intention to give her recipes to someone who would really appreciate them, but I wasn't the one."

"Did she have anyone in mind?" Melinda asked.

Footsteps thudded down the stairs from the second floor. A tall man in his early twenties came into the kitchen with a large basket piled high with neatly folded laundry. He had short brown hair, large hands, and Kaye Lynn's long nose. He also looked like he could muscle through a brick wall without much trouble.

"I'm gonna put my stuff in here so I don't forget it," he boomed, and then caught sight of Melinda. "Oh! Sorry, Mom—I didn't know you had company."

"My son, Gary." Kaye Lynn introduced Melinda and told Gary about the newsletter Melinda was supposedly putting together. "I was just telling her about your grandma Dina's recipes."

Gary set the basket on the floor and cracked his knuckles. The *crunch* nearly rattled the windows.

Melinda flinched and wondered how on earth someone so huge could have come from such a small woman.

"It's nice to know someone's writing up a piece on Grandma Dina," Gary rumbled, pulling up a chair. "I still miss her. I practically grew up in her kitchen. She promised me her *Kletzenbrot* recipe and the others, but she never got around to giving them to me before she died."

"They're for *you*?" Melinda asked, taken aback.

"Gary's quite the baker," Kaye Lynn said. She wrote *die Karotte* on a card. "I think the gene for it skipped a generation."

The young man scratched his chest with thick fingers. He was wearing a faded university T-shirt and old sweats. "Yeah. The guys in my fraternity tried to give me a hard time about it once, but then I threatened to cut them off. Tell a bunch of your frat brothers you won't make them pizza and doughnuts anymore, and next thing you know, the entire chapter is begging on their knees. I'm nowhere near as good as Grandma Dina was, though."

"Why didn't she give you the recipes when you were younger?" Melinda said.

Gary shrugged, and thick muscle moved beneath his shirt. It was like watching a mountain shed an avalanche. "She did give me a couple of them—two cookie recipes and one for Black Forest cherry cake—but she was very protective of the rest. When I was a kid, I think she was worried I might spread them around or something. We made a game out of it—I would try to figure them out, and she would do this elaborate, silly dance to hide what she was doing over the mixing bowl. It always made me laugh. When I got older, I tried making my own stuff. You know, just messing around. It was fun, and I found out that the best part about baking is you get to eat what you make. Want homemade cookies? You can have 'em, hot from the oven, with only twenty minutes' work. It's not hard. And Grandma Dina let me try whatever I wanted. She showed me how to make tricky stuff, like cheesecake, though I always had to get or create the recipes myself."

His eyes went soft and he stared into the distance. "Once when I was about five, I wanted to make those marshmallow cereal squares, but I didn't know how to do it. I knew that you needed cereal and you needed something sticky to hold it together. So I poured some cereal into a bowl and mixed it together with peanut butter. Then I lumped it onto a cookie sheet and put it in the oven at something like four hundred degrees."

"Oh, no!" Melinda laughed. "What happened?"

"It turned into a big, gloppy mess," Gary said. "And I was so disappointed. But the main thing was that Grandma Dina let me try it out, see for myself that it wouldn't work. That year for Christmas, she gave me a basic cookbook. I still have it. She wrote 'Don't ever be afraid to experiment' on the first page. I made real Rice Krispies squares from that book, and they came out pretty good. From then on, I was hooked."

A sinking feeling stole over Melinda. "Were her recipes written down, or did your grandmother keep them in her head?"

"Oh, there was a book, all right," Gary said. "Grandma was a great cook, but her memory was awful, and she wrote everything down. I caught sight of the book once. It was all in German, in that weird old-world script. I couldn't read it, but when Grandma realized I could see it, she snapped it shut and shoved it into her apron pocket. She hid the book somewhere in the bakery every morning when she left work, but no one knew where."

"After Mom died," Kaye Lynn said, writing *der Wein* on another card, "we scoured the bakery for that book, but nothing turned up. We even looked up in the ceiling tiles, but we didn't find it."

"I'd love to have it," Gary put in. His eyes were a little misty. "I could make some of her recipes, like her *Kletzenbrot* or her *Lebkuchen*. It'd be like having her with us again. I think she planned to give it to me when I graduated from high school, but she died in April of my senior year."

Melinda felt a little thrill tingle through her, the same one that always came when she figured out what she needed to do to help a spirit. In order for Dina to cross over, Melinda had to find the recipe book and give it to Gary. No doubt it was still in the dry cleaning store somewhere. All she had to do was convince Jack to let her look for it. Once she did, Gary would get the book, Dina could cross over, and everyone would be happy, including Melinda. Already she was anticipating the emotional high she got from helping a family and settling a ghost. It was one of the things that kept her going, working with difficult and often frightening spirits who—

Dina appeared between Kaye Lynn and Gary. Terror distorted the ghost's face, and she pulled at her face with white fingers that left long runnels in the skin. Her red lips pulled back in an inhumanly wide grimace. Melinda jumped to her feet as Dina reached for Kaye Lynn but stopped just short of touching her.

"Is something wrong?" Kaye Lynn asked with a quizzical look.

"Uh . . . leg cramp," Melinda said feebly. "Had to stand up." She tried to catch Dina's eye, hoping to communicate without words. Dina opened her mouth to scream, but only a faint choking noise escaped from her throat. She clawed at nothing, tore at her hair, stretched her face. The stench of scorched bread invaded the room, and then Kaye Lynn's cards leaped into the air, flinging themselves around the room like giant snowflakes. Kaye Lynn and Gary both jumped to their feet, backing away from the table with mouths and eyes wide open. All the bulbs in the light fixture hanging over the table shattered, showering the table with white glass. White-hot terror flooded through Melinda, raking her nerves and chilling her flesh. It took all of Melinda's willpower to stand her ground. And through it all, Dina kept up her silent scream.

"Stop it!" Melinda ordered. "You have to stop!"

The table flipped over with a crash, sending the rest of Kaye Lynn's materials flying in all directions. Kaye Lynn pressed her back against the wall, obviously confused and terrified. Gary recovered himself. He grabbed his mother and, using his own body to shield her from the chaos, all but shoved her out of the dining room. A hot wind blasted through the room. Cards, string, and bits of glass swirled around Melinda in a deadly blizzard, but she remained where she was.

"What's wrong?" Melinda asked Dina. "I can help you, but you have to tell me. Where's your book?"

Dina stared at her, her mouth gaping wide, her tongue swollen and protruding. Flour rained down from her apron. She raised her head in a scream only she could hear, then vanished. The cards fluttered to the floor. The strings and markers dropped. Broken lightbulbs showered down to form a crunchy layer of glass on the floor. Melinda wrapped her arms around her head until everything had settled, then cautiously emerged, noting with relief that none of the shards had sliced into her.

Drawn by the silence, Gary and Kaye Lynn cautiously peered into the dining room. The place was a shambles. The table lay upside down, its legs sticking up like a dead spider's. Chairs were scattered about, and everything was covered in a layer of broken glass and white cards.

"What the hell was that?" Gary said.

"I don't know," Melinda said, with more truth than lie. "Earthquake?"

"Do we get earthquakes in Grandview?" Kaye Lynn said, surveying the mess. "I don't understand any of this." Something seemed to catch her eye, for she knelt down and plucked a single card from the morass on the floor. Kaye Lynn looked at it, a strange expression on her pale face.

"What is it?" Melinda said.

Kaye Lynn handed her the card. "This . . . this is my mother's handwriting."

On the card in red marker was written a single word in old-world script. "*Darunter,*" Melinda read aloud. "What's it mean?"

"It's German for 'underneath,'" said Kaye Lynn.

4

MELINDA SAT IN bed, pretending to read a copy of *Antique Trader* ("Refinished Tables—Trash or Treasure?") but actually watching Jim undress. This was one of the great pleasures of being married, or at least of being married to Jim. Watching him slide his shirt over his head to reveal broad shoulders, solid muscle, and smooth skin was quite the exercise in sensuality. Jim pulled his pajama bottoms up and climbed into bed beside Melinda as a sigh escaped her. Show over.

"Something wrong?" he asked.

"Nope!" Melinda replied, setting the magazine aside. "Just thinking about how to handle the whole ghostly baker situation. Jack's awfully brittle, and I don't know if he'll let me search his shop for Dina's book, even though Kaye Lynn and Gary couldn't find it. I'm guessing it's underneath something—duh—but what? And where?"

"Maybe you can ask Dina the next time she shows up." Jim lay on his stomach, his head turned toward her, the pillow pushed against the headboard. It looked like an impossibly uncomfortable position for sleeping, but it was the one Jim always favored. Melinda liked knowing that about him.

"Maybe," Melinda said doubtfully. "She doesn't seem inclined to talk much, though, and I can't seem to—"

Terror hammered her into the bed and Melinda was wrenched into a dark room. Candlelight bobbed. Strange voices babbled nonsense. Ghoulish faces leered and floated in blackness. A silver blade glittered. A yellow skull grinned on a table. Pain tore down her every nerve ending with a hot blade. An icy wind chilled her to the marrow. She felt restrained and clawed at the air, trying to escape. Something pulled at her, tore at her, forced her. It was a violation. It was terror.

Melinda tried to understand what she was looking at, but fear paralyzed her mind. She tried to scream. Nothing but a faint choking sound came from her throat. Her mind begged for it to stop, but it went on and on.

A strong smell smashed through her nose, and it tore her away from the place. She gasped and found herself back in bed, her body shivering with cold. The soft sheets and warm blankets around her did little to help the chill. Jim stood over her, concern written across his face.

"You were screaming," he said. "You wouldn't stop. What's wrong? Was it a vision?"

"What was that?" she asked instead. "How did you pull me out of it?"

He held up a small capsule. "Old-fashioned smelling salts. Standard in every EMT's first aid kit. It was all I could think of to do. What happened?"

Melinda shoved the covers aside, got out of bed, and pulled on the first clothes that came to hand. "I think it was Dina. There's something wrong down at her old bakery. She's terrified. I felt it. I need to get down there."

She rushed out of the room before Jim could respond, thudded down the stairs, dashed out the door, and leaped into her SUV. Chilly air blasted from the vents when Melinda turned on the motor, and she slapped the off switch. Downtown Grandview was only a few minutes away, but Melinda felt Dina's terror again. Praying for a complete lack of police surveillance, she floored it. The SUV gave a tiger's roar and tore down the street. Melinda's heart was pounding again, and her hands sweated on the steering wheel as houses and mailboxes rushed past.

Dina flashed into the backseat. *"Help me!"* she screamed, and vanished again just as whirling red and blue lights showed up in Melinda's rear window.

"No," Melinda said. "No nonononononono."

She pulled over, begging any and all powers to have the police officer be responding to some other emergency. He would zoom past her, lights and sirens shouting at the night, leaving her to continue on to her own emergency. But the lights slowed and pulled up behind her. Options flashed through Melinda's mind. She could wait until the officer had exited the car, then take off, giving herself a good head start and a decent chance to lose him. No—he already had her license and would come get her later. Handcuffs would no doubt be involved. She could spin a lie, try to convince the officer to let her go quickly. The problem was, Melinda was a rotten spur-of-the-moment liar. She needed time to think up a decent story, and there was none. For a moment, she found herself wondering if she could show some cleavage and a real big smile, but she discarded that idea almost instantly for a whole host of reasons. Dammit! She pounded her fists on the steering wheel.

In the end, the only option was to wait. The seconds ticked by. She knew the officer was running her plates, checking to see if the car had been reported stolen, looking to see if the owner—her—had a history of assault, an arrest record, or a registered firearm. Meanwhile, she felt Dina's fear long distance. She was fighting for her life, or what was left of it. Melinda had no idea why this was going on; she only knew that a sense of horrible urgency drove her. Every nerve screamed at her to hurry, run, rush. Dina was in pain, needed help. But Melinda forced herself to sit and wait.

At long last, the patrol car door opened. The officer got out, approached Melinda's side of the SUV with a heavy Maglite, and, standing just behind Melinda's line of sight, tapped on the glass. The light partially blinded Melinda as she rolled the window down, forced a smile onto her face, and settled on a strategy: partial honesty.

"I was speeding," she said, still unable to see the officer for the light. "I know. I'm sorry, Officer. It was . . . I'm kind of having a family emergency and I know it's no excuse, but I'm scared and upset and this isn't helping, is it, so I'll shut up now and give you my license."

"And your registration, please," the officer said. It was a woman's voice, harsh and authoritative. Melinda remembered her brief thoughts about flirting, and blushed, even as a new wave of fear from Dina washed over her. Cold sweat popped out across her hairline and her fingers were chilly as she fumbled through her purse. Where was her wallet? Hands shaking at the delay, she turned the purse upside down and spilled its contents across the passenger seat. Pens, notepad, makeup, lipstick, cell phone, breath mints. No wallet. Then she remembered—she'd taken it out of her purse because Jim was short of cash to pay the Chinese food delivery guy. Hadn't she put it back in? Clearly not. Dammit, dammit, dammit!

"I'm sorry, Officer," she said. "I don't have my license with me. I swear I'm not—"

"Please get out of the car, ma'am," the officer said. "Now."

Melinda closed her eyes for a moment, then complied. The police cruiser's lights continued to whirl, shattering shadows with red and blue knives, only to have them re-form behind trees and under gutters. The chilly night air bit through the thin, red T-shirt Melinda had pulled on as she stepped free of the car. *Wrench.* Melinda was standing in a gloomy room. The cloying smell of incense clogged her nostrils. Floorboards creaked. A woman's voice droned. A strange, pale man grinned and beckoned. Pain thundered over Melinda. A powerful white light snapped into existence overhead, seared her with blistering heat. Melinda threw up her hands to shield herself from it. *Wrench.* Melinda was standing back beside her SUV in the cool night air. Her knees went weak and she grabbed at the roof rack for support.

"Are you all right, ma'am?" the officer asked. "Have you been drinking?"

Great, Melinda thought. *Just what I need.*

"No, Officer," she said aloud. "Um . . . head rush. From standing up too fast."

Now that the flashlight wasn't shining in her eyes, she could see the officer clearly. The woman was trim and athletic, one or two inches taller than Melinda, with a businesslike expression and brown hair bound up under her trooper's cap. She wore a brown uniform with beige piping on the collar. Melinda blinked at it.

"No license on you, and there was a problem with your plates when I called them in," the officer said.

"Called them in?" Melinda repeated. No computer in the car, and a uniform that was at least twenty years out of date. Melinda's demeanor changed, and some of the tension drained out of her. "Look, no offense, Officer, but I don't have time for this," she said. "I'm really in a hurry. If I promise not to speed again, can I go? You're doing a fine job, keeping the streets safe and all."

The officer paused for a long moment, then nodded. "All right. But keep it under the limit from here on, got it?"

"Yes, ma'am." Melinda sketched a quick wave, jumped into her Saturn, and sped away. Behind her, the whirling lights vanished as if someone had thrown a switch. Shadows rushed in to fill the empty space. Melinda would have to come back to this stretch of road later, try to help the officer cross over, but right now she had to help Dina. Figuring her chances of encountering another police officer, living or not, were slim, Melinda floored it. Her cell phone slid around on the seat with the other junk from her purse. She snatched it up and dropped it into her lap so it wouldn't get lost and drove like a madwoman.

Downtown Grandview was deserted. Melinda's tires chirped as she pulled up to the dry cleaning store. Leaving the keys in the ignition, she leaped from the car and bolted for the store, shoving her cell phone into her pocket as she went. Plywood covered the broken glass of the front door, but strange lights, green and blue, flickered at the cracks around the edges. Sparks skittered around the door handle. Dina's fear thickened the very air, and Melinda had to physically push through the air in order to reach the shop. When she touched the door, she got a cold shock that rattled her from fingers to toes, as if she had touched electric ice. Fear tightened her stomach, dried her mouth, and she couldn't tell anymore if it was Dina's fear or her own that she felt. Melinda yanked the door open and shouldered her way into the shop.

Chaos swirled around her. Streaking lights whizzed and flicked through the air. A hot wind plucked at Melinda's hair and clothes, and the hair on her neck stood up as if electrified. The clothing racks were empty, and the metal trembled and shuddered. A series of lit candles lined the counter, their flames burning with miraculous steadiness in the wind. Also on the counter was the skull Melinda had seen earlier. Beside the skull was a bronze bowl that rested on a small pillow of red silk and an incense burner that emitted a cloying smoke. Behind the counter stood Wendy King in her slate-gray suit, and in her left hand she held a silver knife. Beside her hovered the male spirit Melinda had seen with Wendy before. His features were indistinct, but he seemed to be rather older, with a fringe of gray beard and a receding hairline. Jack stood nearby, looking frightened but resolute, his gaze fixed firmly on Wendy. Melinda stared. It was the eerie room she had seen in her vision.

Dina flashed into existence beside Melinda. Her features were battered with pain, and her fear, which was now becoming terrifyingly familiar, slammed into Melinda, battering her soul and eating into her mind like acid.

"Stop them!" she screamed. *"You have to stop them! It hurts!"*

"I release you," Wendy intoned from her position near the counter. Her eyes were blank and she seemed to be entranced. "Go into the Light, shining one. By blaze and bell and bowl, I command you. Leave this place!"

With her free hand, she picked up a heavy wooden mallet and struck the bronze bowl. A deep chime rang through the shop. The sound thudded against Melinda's bones and hammered her heart. Dina clapped her hands over her ears and screamed. Another hot gust of oven wind blasted through the shop, but the candles didn't waver.

"I cut your ties to this place," Wendy King chanted. "Go into the Light. You have no more business here." She raised the silver knife, and suddenly Melinda saw it—a single silver thread leading from the shop to Dina. Specifically, it led from a spot behind the counter to Dina. Melinda had never seen anything like it before.

"That light!" Dina shrieked. *"It's so bright! It hurts. It burns!"*

What was going on? Melinda couldn't make sense of any of it, and the terror that infused every inch of the shop, that forced Melinda's heart to pound and her stomach to twist, made it difficult to think. She couldn't concentrate. The spirit next to Wendy placed his hand on hers as a guiding gesture. Wendy didn't seem to be aware of it, but she moved the knife a little to the right so the blade hung directly over the silver thread. She swung it down.

"No!" Melinda shouted, but it was too late. The knife intersected the thread and severed it. Dina howled so loud, Melinda thought her head would split. Pain thundered through Melinda, as if a wet hole had opened in her chest, exposing yellow rib and red muscle. Dina's shrill cry thinned and died away even as her form faded and twisted into nothing. Every candle in the shop went out, plunging the room into shadow. The silence was complete. Melinda could hear crickets chirping outside the shop. She realized she was on her hands and knees on the hard wooden floor. The lack of pain and fear was a relief, but the feeling lasted for only a moment when she remembered its source and forced herself to scramble upright.

"Is it gone?" came Jack's voice in the darkness.

A match flared to life, creating a sphere of yellow light. Wendy's face appeared in the center of it as she lit a candle, then used that one to light a second and a third.

"Your visitor is gone," she said. "For good. But I see we have a second visitor. Melinda Gordon, is that right? You were entering this place when I last left it."

"What did you do to her?" Melinda said through dry, cracked lips.

"What the hell?" Jack said. "How did you get in here?"

Melinda ignored him and crossed the room to confront Wendy across the counter. She knew she had to look a fright, her hair blown in a hundred directions, her hurriedly chosen clothes wrinkled and askew, while Wendy stood looking calm and cool in her pressed gray suit and perfectly formed bun of hair, not a pin or tendril out of place. The spirit Melinda had noticed beside her before was nowhere to be seen.

"Her?" Wendy said. "How do you know the visitor was female?"

"Her name was Dina Mazurek," Melinda said. "She came to Grandview from Germany and opened up a bakery on this spot. She had a family who loved her, but she died before she could pass on her recipe book to her grandson. It was extremely important to her, and that's why she stayed behind. She was a *person,* not a faceless *visitor.*" Melinda all but spat the final word.

"What are you *doing* here?" Jack demanded.

Wendy folded her hands in front of her, confident and serene as a mountain. "The dead have no business in the realm of the living. Sometimes they try to stay behind, and they need encouragement to move on to the next world. They can't stay here. Dina, as you call her, was making life difficult for the living man who owns this shop. Now she is where she belongs."

"Didn't you feel her pain?" Melinda leaned on the countertop, her anger growing at every moment. The skull seemed to grin insolently up at her. "Didn't you *hear* her? She was screaming and begging you not to do this. How could you do something so horrible?"

Jack waved his arms. "Hello! What's going on here?"

"I don't need to see spirits," Wendy said. "I can sense a presence and of course I can see the effects they produce, but seeing spirits—this is a gift that, in my experience, only charlatans possess."

The anger changed to outrage. "Charlatan?" Melinda almost shrieked. "How dare—" And then she cut herself off. She stared at Wendy King as a half-remembered conversation with her grandmother stirred at the back of her mind.

"Oh my God," Melinda said. "You're a medium."

"I'm a spiritual adviser," Wendy corrected.

"What's a medium?" Jack interjected. "This is my shop and I want some answers!"

Melinda didn't take her eyes off Wendy. "She doesn't see spirits like I do. But she can sense them a little and control them to a certain extent. My grandmother told me about people like you. You use tools and paraphernalia that you infuse with your own personal energies to do it. You control ghosts and force them to do what you want. You *make* them cross over, whether they want to or not. Whether they're *ready* or not."

"I bring them to the Light," Wendy corrected. Melinda wanted to plant a fist into that calm, serene expression, and the strength of her reaction surprised her. "They need help, and I give it to them."

"Whether they ask for it or not," Melinda finished. The anger and outrage threatened to boil over, but Melinda forced herself to calm down. No one ever changed his mind by getting yelled at. She kept her voice low and steady. "Wendy, what you do is . . . it amounts to torture. Crossing into the Light is a birthright, and it's not something you can force. It's supposed to be a moment of joy and happiness, of *completion*. I saw what you did with that knife. You slice and slash, and you turn beauty into barbarism. Dina was in terrible pain. Her shining moment, the one she was born to have, was turned into fear and agony." She found tears welling in her eyes and her throat grew thick. "You have to stop this, Wendy. It's cruel, and it isn't right. I can teach you other ways. Even if you can't see spirits yourself, you can help them cross over much more gently. Please. Let me help you."

There was a long pause. Then Wendy sighed and looked at Jack.

"Some people just can't be reasoned with," she said. "It boils down to this: The visitor wasn't ever going to leave your shop. Her way didn't work. Her way left the spirit stranded in the wrong world. My way brought the spirit to its proper place." She produced a large tote bag from beneath the counter and set to packing her materials into it. "I can sense a great deal of spiritual activity in this town. This place has a lot of work for me."

"Who is the spirit that follows you around?" Melinda asked abruptly.

Wendy favored Melinda with another smile and handed her a card. "Call me if you encounter another spirit you can't handle, my dear. I'll be happy to lend a hand."

Melinda's jaw dropped. At that moment, her cell phone chittered in her pocket. Still angry, she yanked it out with too much force and it seemed to jump from her hand. It skittered across the counter, dropped out of sight, and clattered on the floor. Wendy started to lean over for it, but Melinda stopped her.

"Thank you, I'll get it myself," she said with icy politeness, already moving around the counter. She tripped and stumbled as she came around the corner, ruining any hope of continued dignity. The cell phone continued to chitter, then went to voicemail as Melinda bent over to pick it up. The missed calls readout said it was Jim, probably checking to see that she was all right. Melinda blew out a heavy breath.

Wendy, meanwhile, slipped the skull into the tote bag and turned to Jack. She had left the candles on the counter. "We're all done here, Mr. Perry. You can keep the candles—they're only usable once. I guarantee you'll have no more supernatural troubles. If we could just take care of that last matter . . . ?"

"Of course," Jack said quickly. He reached into the back pocket of his jeans, produced a white envelope, and handed it to Wendy King. Wendy opened the flap and briefly glanced at the contents. Melinda caught a flash of green. Money. Nausea roiled through her stomach. On top of everything else, the woman took money. Melinda remembered one time when a man had pressed a hundred-dollar bill on her grandmother when she had crossed over a particularly difficult spirit who had been making life miserable for everyone in his mansion. Grandma's face had tightened, but she had maintained a polite smile when she returned the bill.

"Why didn't you keep it?" Melinda had asked as they drove away together in Grandma's tiny, aging car. "He's rich. To him that was nothing."

Grandma looked shocked, then angry. "If you think you'll ever accept money for this, I'll stop teaching you right this minute, young lady."

Melinda, who was nine, recoiled at her vehemence. "I'm sorry. I didn't mean to make you mad."

"Hmmm." Grandma's expression softened as she drove. "Let me put it this way, dear—how much is your mother worth to you? How much am *I* worth to you?"

"How much?" Melinda blinked, confused. "I don't understand."

"If someone offered you money for me, how much would you take?"

"Nothing!" Melinda said, shocked herself. "You can't give money for a person!"

"Why not? What if someone offered you five million dollars for me to be their grandmother instead of yours. Would you take it?"

The idea both disturbed and horrified Melinda. She would be lost without Grandma. Grandma loved and accepted Melinda exactly as she was, didn't deny her ability to talk to ghosts, listened to what Melinda had to say. She didn't turn Melinda away or shut her out, unlike her mother. Mom never admitted to anything she couldn't see or touch, and sometimes Melinda suspected Mom would be perfectly happy if she could somehow send Melinda to a mental hospital. Life without Grandma would be torture.

"Of course I wouldn't take it!" Melinda said.

"Why not, dear?" Grandma asked. "Five million not enough? Maybe ten, then. Or a hundred."

"A million million isn't enough. A person is priceless!"

Grandma nodded and turned a corner. "That's why we don't charge, dear. Helping a spirit cross over is priceless to both the spirit and to the people left behind. No amount of money would be enough, and any paid amount, no matter how high, automatically makes it cheap."

Melinda stared at the tote bag, heavy with its paraphernalia, as Wendy slipped the envelope and its sickening contents inside. It was like watching someone accept payment for a mafia hit.

"Thank you, Mr. Perry." Wendy caught up her bag and stalked through the store toward the door. Her footsteps echoed in the dead, empty air. The place smelled of stale incense and old clothes now, no hint of flour or sugar. Melinda closed her eyes, hoping that however painful her crossing had been, Dina was now pain-free. A draft of chill night air wafted through the shop as Wendy exited, and the door swung shut. The candle flames danced and the shadows capered.

"Okay, we're done here," Jack said. "You can go."

Melinda jumped. She had forgotten he was there.

"Look, I know you're disappointed," Jack continued. "But I was stuck. My business was failing, I needed to get this thing settled, and you weren't . . . well, it's done now."

Melinda recognized self-justification when she heard it. She also knew that more talk wouldn't change anything. Her heart heavy and hard, she turned to come around the counter—

—and tripped again.

"Sorry," Jack said. "I do that, too, all the time. I think there's a problem with the floor there, but I haven't gotten around to getting it looked at."

But Melinda was already on the floor. She felt around the spot where she had tripped, where she had seen Jack trip. One of the floorboards was uneven. Melinda managed to work a fingernail under it just as Jack came around the side of the counter, the quizzical look on his face transformed into something more ghoulish by the candlelight.

"What the hell are you doing?" he demanded. "Why can't you just get out of my shop and stay out?"

The floorboard popped free, revealing a dark open space. A space beneath. Melinda suspected it was also the spot that had anchored the silver thread. She dipped a hand into the darkness and came up with a leather-bound book. Her heart was pounding again, but heavily, with sorrow instead of excitement.

"What is it?" Jack asked.

Melinda rose and set the book on the countertop. Embossed in the leather was the word REZEPTE.

"I don't speak German," Melinda said, "but it looks an awful lot like the word 'recipe' to me." She opened the book to a random page.

KLETZENBROT

250 ML WASSER, LAUWARM

200 G MEHL, ROGGENMEHL

500 G BIRNE(N), KLETZEN
    (DÖRRBIRNEN)
500 G NÜSSE, GEMISCHT
250 G BACKPFLAUMEN
    (DÖRRZWETSCHKEN)
250 G FEIGEN
250 G ROSINEN
250 G DATTELN

"Can't read this, either," Melinda said, "but yeah—recipe. I'll take this. I just wish I'd found it earlier. Good luck with the dry cleaning, Jack."

Her back rigid, she left the store.

5

IT WAS THE next day, and the recipe book sat on the passenger seat of Melinda's SUV. It made silent accusations as she drove. Melinda tried to ignore it, but the book pulled at her attention, nipped at her, quietly demanded that she look. The weight of it dragged her down, made her hands heavy on the steering wheel.

Outside, an inappropriately cheery sun shone down from a fairy-tale sky filled with nothing but birdsong and clear, clean air. It was early on a Sunday afternoon, and residents of Grandview were taking advantage of the fine early-autumn weekend, mowing lawns one more time before the leaves started to turn, putting away wading pools, playing hide-and-seek, riding bicycles, putting together that last Sunday barbecue. It should have been rainy. It should have been cold. Everyone should have been indoors, playing sad songs on the stereo and drinking sorry mugs of tea without knowing why. Melinda drove slowly, mindful of family cyclists or children who might dash unexpectedly into the street. The book sat dead on the seat beside her.

Melinda could feel the heavy circles under her eyes. Thank God it was Sunday and the antique store was closed—she didn't think she could handle dealing with customers today. Last night she had raged at Jim, then cried on his shoulder, then completely failed to fall asleep beside him. She had spent most of the morning sitting on the front porch, staring at nothing, a cold cup of coffee in her hand. Jim, correctly reading her mood, had left her alone. Melinda hated failing. Not that anyone loved it, she supposed, but this sort of failure was so . . . final. Not every ghost she had worked with had crossed over, but none of them had gone through anything close to what Dina had. The worst thing that had happened to them was that they were still stuck in this world, leaving open the possibility that they could cross over, either on their own or with help from someone else. Even if Melinda hadn't managed to help them, at least she had left knowing it was still possible for it to happen. Dina, however . . . no one could do anything for Dina. She had crossed over in the worst possible way, and there was no way to fix that. Melinda could only try to convince herself that it was Wendy's doing, that it wasn't in any way Melinda's fault.

She wasn't doing a very good job of it.

The SUV pulled up at Kaye Lynn Mazurek's house. Melinda parked, stuffed the book into her purse, and headed up the walk to ring the bell. Her purse felt unaccountably heavy. Seconds later, Gary yanked the door open. His expression told Melinda he was upset about something, and he was clenching beefy fists.

"Gary!" Melinda said. "Is everything all right? Did I come at a bad time?"

"You're Melinda," he said. "That antique lady with the newsletter. Do you know anything about this woman?"

"What woman?"

Wordlessly, Gary stepped aside and pointed into the house. Melinda looked past him. Wendy King, all in gray, was sitting in the living room. Melinda's heart jerked at the sight, and bitter acid sloshed in her stomach. Perched on the edge of a couch across from Wendy was Kaye Lynn, looking uncertain and distressed. Behind the armchair Wendy occupied stood the spirit Melinda had seen with Wendy before. He was tall as a scarecrow, and his straw-blond hair had receded to the back half of his head. Strangely, his outline was a little fuzzy, and Melinda couldn't make out the fine points of his features. He seemed to be wearing brown tweed.

Melinda pushed past an unresisting Gary into the house, her arms folded around her purse like it was a talisman. Kaye Lynn, Wendy, and the spirit all turned to face her, and Melinda felt a slow burn.

"What are you doing here?" she asked Wendy in a dangerously low voice.

"That's between Kaye Lynn and me," Wendy said. "What are *you* doing here?"

Melinda clutched her purse tighter, protecting the contents. No way would she show the book while Wendy King was here. "Also not your business."

Wendy gave Kaye Lynn a small gray smile that looked cast in concrete. "I'm not sure I'd believe whatever she tells you. Melinda here has a way of manipulating people by telling them what they want to hear."

"I'm not sure I know who to believe," Kaye Lynn said. She was clearly miserable, and Melinda's heart went out to her. Gary entered the room and stood in the corner, arms folded like a bodyguard's.

Melinda sat on the couch next to Kaye Lynn. "Listen," she said, "you lost your mother. It was two years ago, but it's not easy to recover from, especially when people come into your house and rake it all up again. I'm really sorry that—"

"I've already told her all that," Wendy interrupted. "I also told her all about her mother's spirit haunting the old bakery. It's a tragedy that she and her son really need to face, and I don't see the point in pussyfooting around the matter."

Melinda let Kaye Lynn's hand go and stared at Wendy. "You told her all that? Just like that?"

"Of course. Mary Poppins may have preferred a spoonful of sugar, but this is life, not a children's movie. Real people want the truth, not a pretty little lie."

"She said that she sent my mother to the other world," Kaye Lynn said. "Is that true?"

Melinda glanced at Wendy again, then at the spirit who stood behind her. A hundred different impulses fought for dominance. She wanted to yank Wendy King into the next room and throttle her. She wanted to yank Wendy King into the next room and interrogate her. She wanted to investigate the spirit who stood behind her. She wanted to comfort Kaye Lynn. She wanted to give Dina's recipe book to Gary. And she wanted to know exactly what Wendy had told Kaye Lynn.

"I believe she did," Melinda said, hedging. "Though I'm not quite—"

"There, you see?" Wendy interrupted. "Melinda was there."

Melinda felt heat rise to her face. "I was just try-ing—"

"Don't be so modest, dear," Wendy interrupted again.

"So you aren't really writing a history newsletter, right?" Gary rumbled from his spot in the corner. "That was a lie?"

Trapped, Melinda decided the only recourse was to come clean. "I was trying to find information about your grandmother, and I didn't think you'd talk to me if I told you her spirit was haunting the site of her old bakery. I was just trying to help. I'm sorry I lied to you."

"Is that why the table went crazy?" Kaye Lynn leaned forward, both hope and pain in her eyes. "Was that my mother?"

"Yes," Melinda replied quietly.

"She's been hanging around the bakery—the dry cleaning store—all this time?"

"I'm afraid so. But Kaye Lynn—" Melinda took the woman's hand again—"she's gone now. She's crossed over."

"Thanks to me," Wendy put in quickly. "As I told you earlier. Melinda's methods are nice, as far as they go, but mine are much more effective. Jack Perry said Melinda worked with your mother's spirit for over two weeks. I crossed her over in less than a day."

"Wait a minute," Melinda said. "Yesterday afternoon when I was here and Dina flipped the table because she was in—because she wanted my attention, that was because of *you*."

Wendy gave that concrete smile Melinda wanted to smack. "Quite likely. I sometimes perform a minor cleansing ritual in a haunted place to see if there's any reaction. I was able to temporarily drive the spirit off the premises."

"And so she came here," Melinda finished.

"I suppose."

Throughout this conversation, the spirit behind Wendy hadn't moved. Now, however, it leaned forward and put its blurred lips to Wendy's ear. Melinda heard the feathery sound of a whisper, mushy and vague. Wendy's eyes went blank. Then she recovered herself. While this was going on, Melinda leaned down as if to adjust her shoe. She slipped the recipe book out of her purse and slid it under the couch.

"This is a little overwhelming," Kaye Lynn said. "I'm not sure I can take this in—or believe it."

"It's all quite true," Wendy said. "Which is why I'm here. My work comes with considerable expenses. I freed your mother from an eternity of pain and difficulty, but it came with a cost." From an inside pocket of her gray jacket, she produced an envelope and handed it to Kaye Lynn. "This is a statement of services. I think you'll find they're quite reasonable, considering what I've given you."

Kaye Lynn stared speechlessly at the envelope. From his corner, Gary came to life. "You want us to pay you?" he said.

"You're a teacher, is that right, Kaye Lynn?" Wendy said, ignoring him.

"Yes," Kaye Lynn said slowly.

"No doubt people tell you all the time that your main payment is the joy you receive in seeing a child learn. But joy doesn't pay the gas bill, does it? It's the same for me. My work is immensely satisfying, but I have expenses of my own to meet. I prefer cash, though I can take a check."

Melinda had been staring in silent outrage. She thought she had seen it all. Ghosts left behind the most amazing secrets, some heart-wrenching, some surprising, some sickening, and Melinda had dealt with just about every possible sort of situation. Like a doctor or paramedic, she had become immune to shock. Or so she had thought. Wendy's audacity and complete lack of empathy shocked Melinda straight to the core.

"This isn't my house, Wendy, " she said at last, "but I think it'd be best if you left now."

"You're right, Melinda. It isn't your house. Perhaps it would be best if you waited outside while we concluded our business."

"This is not a business arrangement!" Melinda realized she was on her feet and that her words had come out as a shout. She clamped her lips together and stared at the floor for a moment. "I'm sorry, Kaye Lynn. We—Wendy and I both—are upsetting your household. And that's wrong of us."

"Please leave now," Kaye Lynn said. Her soft voice was firm. "Both of you. I want you out of my house. And take this with you." She crumpled up the envelope into a ball and threw it at Wendy. "Go. Now!"

Wendy let the ball of paper drop to the floor. "Kaye Lynn, I don't think you understand the—"

"I don't recall giving you permission to call me by my first name, Ms. King," Kaye Lynn said, still firm. "You just started using it to give yourself an air of false intimacy. I teach high school, and I know all the tricks people play. Gary, would you show both these ladies the way out?"

Gary strode like a mobile oak tree toward Wendy, who got up and backed toward the front door. Melinda didn't blame her. The blurry spirit shot Melinda a look, then vanished. She followed the enormous Gary as he herded Wendy out of the house while Kaye Lynn walked into the kitchen without looking back. Melinda felt as if an icicle had replaced her spine. Gary banged the door open and made a firm gesture with one thick arm. Wendy actually stopped in the threshold.

"You're a reasonable young man," she said. "Maybe you could talk with your mother and—"

Gary cracked his knuckles. "Out."

Wendy stiffened and marched out the door. Melinda suppressed a smile. She herself also paused when she reached the door. "Look under the couch," she murmured, and went outside.

Wendy was crossing the street toward a red Saturn Sky, her hard shoes slamming the concrete like little jackhammers beneath the autumn sunlight. Melinda dashed to catch up.

"What are you doing?" she demanded. "Are you *trying* to hurt them?"

"Don't be a child, dear," Wendy said. "Life is for the living. The dead try to leech off us. They feed off our energy, drain us, and it's the job of people like us to get rid of them. It's a job like any other, and we're right to demand recompense. Anything else is naïve."

"I don't even know where to *start* with that," Melinda cried. "Why are you even here, Wendy? What are you doing in Grandview?"

"Grandview has a high spiritual activity index," Wendy said. Her face wore that implacable, smooth expression. "I'm needed here and might set up permanent shop. Afraid of a little competition?"

"I'm worried that you're hurting people instead of helping them." Melinda's voice rose along with her anger. She couldn't seem to help it. "You aren't crossing ghosts—you're forcing them. You're not helping people—you're causing them pain. And then you *charge* them for the privilege."

They were standing in the middle of the street. A light breeze poured over both of them, bringing the fresh scent of autumn leaves. Two houses down, a woman was raking leaves with a rhythmic shushing of her rake while two kids rode tricycles on the sidewalk in front of her. Wendy patted Melinda on the cheek. Melinda jerked back and almost bit her hand.

"Still a child," Wendy said. "Reality hasn't touched you yet, I can see."

"Who's the spirit that follows you around?" Melinda asked abruptly.

Wendy gave her the same concrete smile she had before. "My father is always with me. I can sense his presence. He guides me in everything I do."

Her father. A dozen thoughts flashed through Melinda's head, but all of them were questions. Why was he following Wendy around? Why hadn't he crossed over? Was he responsible for her mercenary attitude? He'd whispered something in her ear right before she'd presented Kaye Lynn with her little statement, after all. Had he been a medium, too?

She decided to go with the obvious question. "Why haven't you crossed him over?"

The look Wendy gave her was at once condescending and pitying. "He's my spirit guide. He's my conduit from this world to the next. I couldn't help other spirits without him."

"I thought you couldn't help other spirits without a Visa card," Melinda found herself saying.

"You have a lot of anger in you," Wendy observed. "Perhaps when you learn to let go of it, child, you'll be more effective as a spiritualist."

With that, she got into the red Sky and drove away, leaving Melinda speechless in the middle of the street. She stood there until a car honked, startling her and making her jump back. A pair of heavy arms entangled her. Melinda squeaked and struggled to get away. Gary stepped back as the car drove past.

"Sorry," Gary said. "I didn't know you were going to jump into me like that."

"Gary. Hi." Melinda shook her head, trying to regain her composure. "What—?"

He held up the recipe book. His eyes were large and soft. "You brought this and stuck it under the couch. Where did you get it?"

"I found it at the dry cleaning store underneath a loose floorboard," Melinda said. "I thought you'd want it, but I didn't want to give it to you when Wendy was there."

Abruptly Melinda found herself crushed in a huge hug and the air rushed out of her. It was like being embraced by Mount Everest with oak-tree arms. Then the mountain was gone and she could breathe again.

"Sorry, sorry," Gary said, stepping back and blushing. "I just—we've been looking for this for so long. Mom can translate these, and I can make some of Grandma Dina's stuff for Thanksgiving and Christmas and . . . well, it means a lot. Thank you." He turned and fled for the house.

"You're welcome," Melinda called to empty air. Okay, that made her feel at least a little better. Not perfect, but a little. She turned back to her SUV.

"It's not just what she's doing," Melinda said to Andrea, "but how she's doing it."

It was the same Sunday, but later, and the two women were back at the Ray house in the front parlor. With the store closed, it was a good time to catalog the house's enormous stash of antiques. Now that Andrea and Melinda were business partners, there was no need for Melinda to bribe Andrea with double pay for working on a Sunday. It was actually quite pleasant, working in the creaky old house, with its smells of sawdust and new paint and the thumping footsteps of men on the floors above—Jim had come along to see the place, and Kevin had roped him into helping with something involving pipes and a welding torch.

Andrea's camera flashed, and Melinda scribbled more notes on her pad: *Edwrdn sfa red vlvt clw ft sml rip excnlt cndtn.* Andrea had urged her to get a BlackBerry or even bring along her laptop, but although Melinda was quite conversant with computers, she found BlackBerries a little awkward, and a laptop was just too clunky to move from spot to spot. Andrea had brought her own laptop, but she was wielding the camera. So for the moment, it was back to pen, paper, and Melinda's illegible shorthand.

"You mean it's that Wendy takes money for what she does," Andrea said.

"That, and the torture and the pain." Melinda scribbled some furious notes over a footstool. "How many spirits has she ripped apart like this? It makes me want to cry and throw up and scream all at once."

"She sounds horrible," Andrea replied staunchly. "I'd want to . . . what's the ghost-chaser equivalent of ripping someone's lungs out with a spoon?"

"Andrea!" Melinda said, pausing in her work. "I wouldn't want to do something like that!"

"Of course not." Andrea sniffed. "It would create another ghost for you to cross over. But I'm the best friend in this picture, so I'm allowed to say things you're not in order to make you feel better."

"The only thing that'll make me feel better is watching her backside retreat far into the distance." Melinda wrote more notes: *ND tbl 3 lgs oak fine cndtn 1850?*, then paused. "Actually, that's not true. Her leaving town would just move the problem somewhere else. I don't know what to do about her, Andrea. That's what bothers me the most."

"Who says you have to do anything?" Andrea countered. "You don't have to solve every problem. No one appointed you caretaker of the world."

"If I don't, then who? And don't you dare say the Ghostbusters."

"Heaven forbid." The camera flashed. "But the entire world doesn't rest on your shoulders, and it won't come apart if you don't remove every single thorn in it."

Melinda found herself bristling. "So I should stop trying?"

"That's not what I said," Andrea replied, calmly taking another picture. "I'm telling you that you don't need to beat yourself up for not being able to help everyone."

"Sorry." Melinda twitched a dust cover aside to reveal another end table. "I guess I'm just a little on edge."

Jim appeared in the parlor doorway. His face was pale and he pointed toward the staircase behind him with a shaky hand. "Uh . . . there's . . . er . . . I mean . . . you . . ."

Melinda set the pad down. "I'll be right up."

"I think I'll stay down here," Andrea said. "Suddenly I'm in the mood to be bored for a while."

Melinda and Jim tripped quickly up the creaky stairs, Melinda in the lead. "I'm surprised you saw anything. Adults can't see most ghosts."

"I didn't see so much as . . . I don't know," Jim said behind her. "I was walking down that hallway and . . . I just wanted to leave. I was sweating and scared and . . . I think I would have thrown up if

I had stayed longer. And the shadows kept moving at the corner of my eye. It was nasty stuff."

They arrived at the beginning of the hallway. Melinda peered down its darkened length. It lay there like a black serpent daring her to come closer. The darkness stirred. Something was staring back at Melinda. She sensed cold, hostile eyes examining her, staring through her and taking her measure. It made her feel cold and naked. Midway along the hallway, a closet door creaked open by itself, then softly clicked shut. Jim gasped and backed up a step. Goose pimples crawled over Melinda's skin, but she held her ground.

"What's Kevin doing?" she asked without taking her eyes off the dark.

"He's still up on the third floor dealing with the sink. I came down for beer. There's a law that you can't do plumbing work without . . . without . . ." His eyes wandered toward the hallway and he trailed off, his bravado drained by the blackness ahead of them.

"I know you're there," Melinda called softly. "Come on out. I can help you."

The darkness swallowed Melinda's words, leaving not even an echo behind. Melinda took a tentative step forward. Sudden terror whitened her knuckles and froze her in midstep. The long runner on the floor trembled like an eager serpent's tongue, and the darkness became a maw, ready to swallow her alive. Melinda took a step backward and bumped into Jim. His flesh was cold and slick with sweat.

"Let's leave," he whispered hoarsely.

But Melinda forced herself to shake her head. "Not yet. He's afraid. We're feeling his fear."

"Are you sure?" Jim's voice cracked. "Because it feels like mine."

"He can't hurt you." But there was no conviction in Melinda's voice. Down that hallway lay every nightmare, every bit of black childhood terror that had chased her up a cellar stair or through an attic or out of a dream. Her hair felt damp, her armpits soggy.

"It's not real," she said aloud. She had meant to say it in a firm voice, but the words came out hoarse and scratchy. "It's nothing to be afraid of. It can't hurt us."

"Then why do I feel like I'm going to fall off a cliff if I walk down that hall?" Jim whispered. "We should go, but I'm not leaving until you do."

Melinda took a step forward again. Her feet were granite lumps, her hands blocks of ice. A second step. She touched a toe to the worn blue runner and flinched, expecting the serpent's tongue to rise and wrap around her. It didn't move. A third step. Her body grew chilly now, and she could see her breath. The cotton blouse and simple slacks she was wearing felt thin. Melinda hugged herself, arms tight around her waist to ward off the cold and the darkness that pressed around her now. Dimly, she was aware of Jim walking behind her. His breathing was harsh and ragged, and her own heartbeat was a quick, thin rhythm in her ears.

"Hello?" she whispered. "I just want to help you. You don't need to be afraid."

She reached for the light switch on the offhand chance it would work. A hard hand closed over her wrist, and she yelped.

"Don't," Jim said, letting her go. "Kevin told me that the electricity on this floor started acting up this morning. Bad idea to touch the lights."

Melinda nodded, then turned back to the horrid hallway. She took two brisk steps and reached the closet door. The darkness was nearly absolute now. It was like hanging in space. The fear had lessened after Jim had released her hand. Maybe touching him—

The closet door slammed open and whacked her in the face. Melinda screamed as pain slammed into her nose and left cheek. She doubled over, hands on her face. The door banged shut and Melinda felt Jim's firm hands on her shoulders. He pulled her away, down the way they had come, and into the light.

"Are you all right?" he said in his EMT voice. "Let me see."

It was hard to take her hands away from her face. She felt like a three-year-old who had taken a spill and wanted to cover the wounds. But she did as Jim said, blinking in the light of the stairwell. Her face throbbed with tight, hot pain, and she could feel swelling coming on. Blood dripped from her nostrils. Jim examined her face without touching it, his blue eyes inches from her own and filled with concern.

"Your nose isn't broken," he said, putting an arm around her, "but you're going to have a nasty bruise on your cheek. Let's get some ice on it, quick! In the kitchen. I'll see if Kevin has some ibuprofen for the pain and swelling. If not, I'll get the first aid kit in the truck. Pinch your nose for the bleeding. Don't tip your head back—you might get blood in your lungs."

At that moment, Kevin came down the stairs from the third floor. He had gray putty in his sunset hair and his flannel shirt was streaked with grease. "What's going on? Is everything all right?"

"A little accident," Jim said, herding Melinda down to the first floor.

"Rad idto a door id the dark," Melinda added. Her voice was thick because she was pinching her nostrils shut. Pain continued to throb in her cheek and nose. "Doe big deal. Do you hab ice?"

A few minutes later, she was sitting at the kitchen table with an ice pack on her face, two tablets of ibuprofen in her stomach, and a mug of tea at her elbow. She was still pinching her nose.

Kevin and Jim had been ordered back upstairs on the grounds that hovering menfolk wouldn't speed Melinda's recovery any. Andrea sat with her at the table, her laptop out so she could upload pictures, transcribe some notes, and check her e-mail.

"A cell modem is a fine thing to us tech junkies," she said. "We can babysit the wounded and accomplish useful labor at the same time."

"I'b dot wounded," Melinda protested.

"Uh-huh. When you want makeup tips on hiding that bruise, let me know." Andrea peered at her screen. "Oooo! The historical society got back to me faster than I thought."

Melinda shifted the ice pack. When she left it on, it was too cold. When she took it off, her face got too hot. "About what?"

"The Ray family. There wasn't anything about them online, so I contacted the county historical society. You keep that ice pack on your face and I'll read."

"Doe."

"You sound like Homer Simpson. I'll take that to mean *go*. Let's see. Hey—pictures." Andrea's eyes tracked back and forth as she skimmed photos and read text. Melinda sat in the hard kitchen chair, trying to rein in her impatience. She hated getting information through someone else's filter. Who knew what minor yet critical point Andrea might fail to mention because it seemed too trivial

to her? Life was full of points like that—bits of
information that seem insignificant but later turn
out to be keystones in the arch or fulcrums for
the lever. But there was nothing for it here. Melinda was in no shape to operate a computer, and
it was Andrea's e-mail account in any case. She'd
ask Andrea to forward her the full contents of the
file later.

Andrea raised surprised eyebrows at what she
saw on the screen. "Huh. I had no idea the Rays
were so well connected. You wouldn't know it by
looking around town today."

"Wad does dat mean?"

"Check this out." She turned the computer
so Melinda could see the screen. It was a map of
Grandview and Driscoll County. A good chunk of
the area was colored red.

"This is a map from the eighteen hundreds,"
Andrea said. "The red area is Ray land. The family owned most of Grandview. Not only that, the
historical society said that most of the buildings
in Grandview were originally built by a company called Ray Construction. The company was
founded by Frederick Ray."

"Huh. I'b nebber heard ub dem."

"Me, either. But if this house is any indication,
the family's fallen on hard times. The plat books
say the only thing in the Ray name these days is
this house and the land right around it."

Melinda took a sip of tea. It had cooled a bit and was easier to drink. Then she pinched her nose again and reapplied the ice pack to her face. Jim had told her to keep the ice on her face for as long as she could stand it to minimize the bruising and swelling. The cold was uncomfortable, but she didn't want a swollen knot on her face.

"A little more recently," Andrea continued, spinning the computer back around, "we have Arthur Ray."

Melinda leaned forward in sudden excitement, then winced as the motion rubbed the ice pack against her tender skin. "Uncle Arthur?"

"Seems likely. The newspaper article here—it's dated 1925—reports a construction accident on a Ray Construction building site. A boiler blew up and killed a man named Arthur Ray. He was the son of Frederick and Regina Ray and the brother of Florence Ray."

"Kebbin's Grandma Florence," Melinda said. "Her brudder was damed Arthur."

"Mmmm-hmm. And check this out. In the same year, Frederick Ray contracted smallpox and died."

"Smallpox?"

"This was in the days before compulsory vaccination," Andrea reminded her. "Back then, smallpox had a high death rate. The people who didn't die were often scarred."

"I know." Melinda set the ice pack aside for a moment and stopped pinching her nose. Her speech cleared. "I've helped Grandma cross over a few smallpox casualties."

"Not fun. The article the historical society sent me says Florence nursed her father until the end, but the disease took him anyway."

Melinda drank more tea. The ibuprofen was kicking in and her injuries were starting to feel better. "She didn't catch it herself?"

"The article doesn't say, but I'm guessing not, since she lived to that ripe old age Kevin envied. How did she get elected to take care of Daddy? I mean, this is a disease that killed a lot of people. You'd think Frederick wouldn't *want* his daughter around in case she got it, too. They were rich. Why not hire someone?"

"Maybe she volunteered. Maybe she wanted to do it herself."

"Or maybe he made her," Andrea said darkly.

"Andrea! That's awful!"

Andrea snorted and folded her arms. "Like that's the worst thing either of us has ever seen."

"Well, no, but why start out assuming the worst?"

"Because things can only get better when you do." She stretched and moved her head around, popping her neck. "I'll forward you the material so you can read it all."

"I'm trying to get a time line straight in my head," Melinda said. "The Ray family arrives in the eighteen hundreds and buys a lot of land in and around what eventually becomes Grandview. Eventually, Frederick Ray starts a company called Ray Construction that puts up a lot of the buildings in Grandview. His son Arthur—who I assume works for Daddy Frederick's company—is working at one of the construction sites when a boiler blows up and kills him. This is in 1925. Then Daddy Frederick catches smallpox. Florence, for whatever reason, tries to nurse him back to health, but he dies."

Andrea held up a forestalling hand. "Nuh-uh. Got it wrong, but it's my fault. I gave the information wrong. Frederick's obituary is dated April 1925. Arthur's boiler blew up in May of the same year."

"So Father Frederick contracts smallpox, then Brother Arthur dies in the boiler accident a month later," Melinda said. "What a tragedy. This poor family! I wonder if that's why Florence never left the house. Her father and her brother dead of horrible causes in less than a year. How do you cope with that?"

"No idea," Andrea said. "And I hope I never have to find out."

"What about Florence's mom?"

"Already gone. Died giving birth to Florence."

Melinda bit her lip. "Ouch. How much do you want to bet Florence was the woman of the house, then? Mother to everyone from the time she was big enough to cook and clean and sew."

"In this house? Servants, my dear. Servants."

"Point." She put the ice pack, now getting wet and squishy, back on her cheek. "Anything else in there?"

"That's it." Keys clicked beneath Andrea's fingers. "But the historical society lady said she could keep digging if I want. Do I want?"

"How much does it cost?" Melinda asked warily.

"Nothing. The society is run by women like you—they want to help. The only difference is, they're retired and have more time."

"Then we definitely want. Forward me the stuff you have so far, will you?"

More keys clicked on the laptop. "Done! Want to get back to those antiques? We're nearly finished with the downstairs."

"Nope." Melinda set the ice pack down and rose from the table. "I have a job on the second floor."

"Dropped something," Andrea said, pointing at the floor and ruining a faintly dramatic moment. Melinda, feeling slightly put out, looked down. A bit of cardboard stared up at her. Wendy's card. Melinda frowned and a bit of annoyance flickered through her.

"It's just a piece of trash." She snatched it up, glared at the blocky writing, then marched over to the open kitchen wastebasket and dropped it in. It fluttered down like a dead insect. "I cast thee out," she said.

"And they call me the weird one."

"I'll ignore that. For now, I'm going up to have another chat with Uncle Arthur."

Andrea got up, too. "I'll go with you."

"No, stay down here and keep up with the antiques." Melinda ran a finger over her cheek and winced. "I think he might be more talkative if I'm alone."

6

THIS TIME MELINDA brought a flashlight. A mega-powerful, steroid-fed flashlight. With new batteries. And an unbreakable lens. You could shine deer with it and then club them down with the handle. It always amazed Melinda how many people in books or movies seemed to possess flashlights with batteries that conveniently died when a little darkness would make the moment scarier. Not here.

And this time, Melinda built some momentum to overcome the fear-filled corridor. She tapped firmly up the stairs to the second floor. She strode firmly down the forbidden hallway. She switched the flashlight firmly on and blasted the hallway shadows into oblivion. The corridor leaped into a full blaze of brilliance. The faded runner turned so pale, it looked more beige than blue.

"Come on out," she said. "I know you're here. I just want to talk."

Nothing. The flashlight continued to blaze in the hallway, illuminating every cornice, floorboard, and speck of dust. No sign of the ghost. Melinda blew out an exasperated sigh. The light might be keeping the spirit away, but after the last encounter, she didn't feel inclined to shut it off. She wished she knew a magic word or gesture, something that would bring a spirit out of hiding like a genie pulled from a lamp.

"Look, I know you can hear me. I just want to talk. I'm not going to hurt you. I'm—"

"Hello? Who are you talking to?"

Melinda spun and aimed the flashlight at the voice behind her. The illumination slammed into a short, slender woman who was carrying a small child. The beam washed all color out of her skin and hair, making her look like a spirit, though Melinda could see she was quite alive. The child looked strange—stiff. As the light struck them, the woman gasped in pain and spun around with the child still in her arms.

"Ow!" the child yelped.

"Sorry!" Melinda shut off the flashlight. Instantly, the hallway plunged into absolute blackness. Melinda blinked, trying to regain her night vision. The darkness pressed in around her, thick and heavy as a dungeon. A cold feeling stole over her, eyes cold as ice staring at the back of her neck.

"Better," the woman said in the darkness. "Are you the antiques lady? My husband Kevin mentioned you'd be around."

"Oh! Yes, that's me," Melinda said a little too cheerfully. Her eyes were beginning to adjust, and she could make out the woman's silhouette in the dim light. So far the child in her arms hadn't spoken. Something shifted with a soft creak behind Melinda, and the icy feeling moved, as if the eyes were glaring down at her from above. The woman stepped forward. Melinda felt split in two, trying to deal with the strange woman but needing to keep a mental eye on the spirt hovering around her.

"I'm Sally Ray," the woman said. "And this is Andy."

"Hi," piped the child. Melinda's eyes had adjusted a bit more and she saw the kid give a stiff sort of wave.

"Hello." Melinda automatically put out a hand, then realized the woman's hands were full. The child reached out to shake instead. Melinda touched lumpy cloth instead of the soft skin she had been expecting, and she jerked her hand back with a horrified cry.

"Don't be scared," the child said. "I won't bite. I don't even have teeth."

"Uh . . . oh . . ." Melinda floundered for words. "I didn't . . . I wasn't expecting . . ."

Sally Ray gave a light laugh and stepped back a little. Melinda's eyes had fully adjusted now, and she could see the "child" was actually a large male puppet with a pale felt face, brown yarn hair, and blue overalls. One of Sally's hands was slipped into the puppet's head from behind, and her other hand maneuvered a stick that was connected to one of the puppet's wrists.

"You're jumpy," the puppet said, though Sally didn't try to hide the fact that she was providing the voice. "You act like you've never seen a kid before."

"Andy," Sally said to the puppet in her own voice, "I've told you before—you aren't real. You're just a puppet. You can't even move your right arm."

"I can't?" Andy's left side twitched, but the arm, which had no stick for Sally to control, didn't move. "I can't move my arm!"

"That's what I've been trying to tell you," Sally said. "Why don't you run upstairs like a dear and play while I talk to this lady, all right?"

"I can't!" Andy wailed.

"Why not?"

"I'm just a puppet!"

At that, Andy went limp. A little confused and put off, Melinda decided the best thing to do was applaud. She could still feel the cold eyes on her from above.

"Thanks," Sally said, pulling her hand free of the puppet. "I'm not really insane. It's just a little fun."

"That's a professional-looking puppet," Melinda said. "Do you do this for a living?"

"Sure do," Sally said. "I worked on a couple kids' shows for years, and then on Broadway for a while for a musical. But the night life got tiring, and then I met Kevin, and he wanted to live in Grandview. So now I make puppets and sell them online."

The icy eyes continued to stare. Melinda's instincts told her to leave, get out, run. Goose bumps stippled her skin, and the hallway temperature dropped several degrees. Sally didn't seem to notice.

"Does everyone make their living online these days?" Melinda said weakly. The eyes moved closer in the darkness. Melinda switched the flashlight back on and set it on the floor so that the powerful beam shone straight up. The indirect light lit the hallway and chased the shadows away without blinding the two women, and Melinda felt the eyes retreat, though they didn't disappear entirely. "I swear I'm the only retailer who doesn't."

Sally grinned, and now that the light was back, Melinda could see how very beautiful she was. Her enormous blue eyes, small, upturned nose, and smooth, fair skin made Melinda think of one of the antique dolls Andrea had taken from the closet farther down the hallway. Her short brown hair was fetchingly cut to accent her fine features. Her hands, however, were strong and wiry. The muscles and tendons stood out like wires as she set Andy down on the floor. The puppet sat limply, like an unconscious child. Melinda shivered, though she couldn't sense the cold eyes anymore. Had the ghost withdrawn?

"The Internet," Sally said. "Without it, my puppet business couldn't survive in a place like Grandview, and that would suck because I love this house. I already put my workshop up in the attic because it gives me three times the space I used to have. I just finished Andy here, in fact, and I was taking him for a test run when I saw you. How're the antiques coming?"

"Good. We'll be putting the first batch on sale at the store tomorrow." Melinda cocked her head, interested despite herself. "Do you sell a lot of puppets?"

"Oh, sure. There's a big call for them, especially for churches and stuff. They do a lot of Bible stories for kids. I make a dozen David and Goliaths a month."

The shadows stirred and Melinda shivered again. On the floor beside Sally, Andy slowly got to his feet. He looked up at Melinda and opened his mouth wide. A pink, heart-shaped tongue was glued to the inside surface. Melinda's stomach turned to water. He took an experimental step toward Sally on soft, silent shoes. Sally hadn't seen him yet.

"Do you think the antiques will sell well?" Sally was asking. "Kevin seems enthusiastic, but he gets that way about new projects. I wonder a little if this B-and-B thing will peter out."

Andy took another step. He wobbled, then regained his balance, as if learning to walk as he went. His felt fingers reached into the pocket of his overalls and pulled out a pair of scissors. The blades gleamed silver and sharp in the hard beam of the flashlight.

"Look out!" Melinda snapped.

Sally spun and Andy lunged. With a shout, Sally jumped aside. The scissors slashed empty air.

"Run!" the puppet growled in a voice made of dust. "Leave! Go!" It crouched, then sprang at Melinda like a cat. It landed on her front, gripping her blouse with one pink hand and raising the scissors with the other. Fear stabbed through her even as the ridiculousness of the situation registered. She tried to pull Andy away, but the puppet was surprisingly strong and felt ropy as a snake. It brought the scissors down toward Melinda's neck. Melinda flinched, readying herself for slashing, bloody pain, but another hand caught the puppet's wrist. Sally's. The other woman pulled with obvious effort, her face a frightened mask in the strange illumination of the flashlight. The scissors moved away from Melinda's neck.

"It's empty!" the puppet hissed. "Go! Leave!"

"These are *my* scissors!" Sally snarled, and she yanked hard. Abruptly Andy let go. He twisted in Sally's grip, surprising her. She screamed as the scissors scored her forearm. Andy dropped to the floor and scuttled toward Melinda, who instinctively backed away.

"Stop this!" she said. "Arthur, if that's you, you need to stop!"

"Get out of here!" Andy hissed, swinging the scissors like a knife. "I'll hurt you!"

Sally held her injured forearm and stared at the scene in disbelief. "What the hell is going on?"

Melinda aimed a kick at Andy, but he dodged and ran. Melinda thought he was trying to get past her for the back stairs, but instead he grabbed the flashlight. The world exploded into retina-blasting whiteness as the puppet aimed the beam straight into her face. Hot pain stabbed her eyes. Melinda flung up her hands to shut out the awful brightness. Adrenaline hummed in every nerve and vessel. Being blinded in the hall felt like being trapped in a cage with a rabid animal. She felt exposed, vulnerable as a kitten. Any moment she expected to feel a blade slash at her, peel her skin away like the surface of a ripe plum. Wildly she tried kicking again, but her feet met only air. The light faded to red, and Melinda blinked furiously, trying to clear her vision.

A soft weight landed on her back. Melinda screamed and grabbed at it, but the puppet twisted in her grip. She managed to get her arm up and something crashed into it. Pain smashed the bone. Melinda grunted. The puppet had hit her with the flashlight. Cold metal pressed against her throat. Melinda froze. Her vision began to clear and she could see shadows now.

"Don't!" she gasped. "Arthur, you can't."

"Leave!" Andy's dusty voice snarled at her. "The grave is empty! You have to leave!"

Abruptly, the metal left Melinda's neck. She could make out Sally standing near her, struggling with Andy. There was a tearing sound, and the puppet's arm came off. The scissors clattered to the floor. Melinda managed to reach around, grab hold of the puppet, and yank hard. Andy flew through the air and hit the corridor wall with a squashy *thump*. The puppet hung there for a moment, his glossy white eyes staring at Melinda. Then Andy fell to the threadbare runner, where he lay faceup and motionless. Pale stuffing leaked out of his torso at the shoulder where the arm was missing. Sally stared down at it.

Melinda realized she was panting. She forced her breathing to a more normal level, then searched the floor until she found the flashlight. Her arm throbbed dully. She would have another lovely rainbow bruise tomorrow to match the one on her face.

"Are you all right?" she asked Sally.

"I'm bleeding," Sally said, holding up her own arm. Blood trickled from a long, shallow cut. "But it's nothing some washing and direct pressure can't handle. Did you—?"

Footsteps thundered across the hall above and rushed down the steps. Kevin, Jim, and Andrea appeared in the corridor, all talking at once and wanting to know what was going on. Both men led their wives away from the corridor, though Sally insisted on collecting both the scissors and the mangled puppet first and taking them with her.

"I told you, Kevin," Sally said as the four of them headed down into the kitchen. "I *told* you."

Jim got some water going in the sink and Andrea made another ice pack while Kevin, his face set like wood, pulled clean kitchen towels from a drawer and pressed one to Sally's cut. "Not now," he muttered.

"What, do you think Melinda didn't see it? My puppet came to *life*, Kevin. We both saw it."

"Told you what?" Melinda asked, pulling out a chair at the table and sitting down. The "dead" puppet lay on the table beside the scissors and an open first aid kit. Melinda carefully moved the scissors out of the puppet's reach, just in case.

Sally turned to her. "We have a ghost in the house."

Silence fell across the kitchen. Both Jim and Andrea looked at Melinda. Kevin turned his back, busying himself with some small task at a cupboard and refusing to look around. Now that the words had actually left her, Sally seemed to wish she could take them back. She sat in a chair across from Melinda, still holding the towel to her arm. Melinda, caught off-guard, didn't know quite how to react. Usually in these situations she had to persuade people of two things: that ghosts existed and that one was hanging around. Her other common option was to try to cross the ghost over without letting anyone know what was going on. Having someone tell *her* there was a ghost was a new experience. Andrea handed her the ice pack and she pressed it to her bruised arm.

"Yes," Melinda finally said. "You definitely have a ghost."

Kevin thumped a bottle of scotch on the cupboard and slopped some of the clear brown liquid into a glass. He held the bottle out to the rest of the room, but there were no takers. Tension rode his body, and Melinda tightened her jaw. She'd have to defuse Kevin before she could go any further, but he was clearly going to retreat into stubborn disbelief. "Look, just because I told you that stupid story about what supposedly happened to me and my sister at that one Thanksgiving doesn't mean—"

"Do you think I cut myself, Kevin?" Sally interrupted. "I'm *bleeding*, for God's sake."

"So you slipped," he said. "It happens."

"It's nothing to be ashamed of," Melinda said quietly. "And it's all right to be scared."

The moment the words left her mouth, Melinda realized they were a mistake. Kevin's blue eyes grew icy and hard. Melinda's heart sank. She had called out his fear and embarrassed him in front of his wife and three strangers. Kevin stared at her for half a second, then snorted in disdain and slugged down a mouthful of scotch. "I'm not scared."

"I am," Jim said from the sink.

Kevin turned toward him. "Yeah?"

"Damn right. Something I can't see or touch just attacked my wife, and I don't know what to do about it. What if it happens again and I can't defend her?" Jim finished washing his hands and crossed the kitchen to Sally. "Let me see that cut. The bleeding should be under control, but I want to be sure. Anyway, Kevin, any sane man would be afraid of what's going on here. Melinda deals with this stuff all the time and it scares the hell out of me because I almost never know how to help her. It's not fair, but that's the way it is, you know?"

Kevin's expression softened a little bit and he edged warily toward the table, drink still in his hand. Andrea looked like she wanted to say something, but Melinda shot her a silencing look.

"She deals with this a lot?" Kevin said.

"Oh yeah." Jim lifted the towel and examined Sally's cut. The bleeding had indeed stopped, and he gently wiped the drying blood away. "It's some kind of family gift. She can see ghosts and stuff that normal people can't."

Melinda was about to protest Jim's use of the word *normal* in this context, but Andrea stepped on her foot and she said nothing. Jim continued working on Sally's cut, spreading antibiotic ointment on it and covering it with a loose bandage. Melinda saw what was going on. Jim was subtly pointing out to Kevin that the two men were in the same position, that they had failed to rescue their endangered wives, and that they were both shaken by the experience, but Jim was dealing with it and could cop to it, making it all right for Kevin to do the same. Jim's care of Sally also put Kevin into Jim's debt, subtly requiring him to go along with Jim, allowing him to do so without losing face. It was a neat trick, one that Melinda couldn't have pulled off, and it saved her enormous difficulty. She gave Jim a grateful look that promised him special treats later. He gave her a quick smile in return.

"She can help, if you want her to," Jim finished. "She'll figure out why the ghost is hanging around and persuade it to move on. It's what she does. You can say no—it's your house—but you probably won't find a lot of guests who'll want to stay on a floor where a poltergeist or whatever tries to stab them under their down comforters."

Kevin slugged down the rest of the scotch. "You've got a point. It's just . . . I don't like talking about it. It's weird. I don't even know why I told that stupid Thanksgiving story."

"It *is* weird," Jim said. "No question. But think of it this way—you have just one ghost to get rid of. I've gone through this dozens of times."

"Hey!" Melinda said, at last pushed too far. "Who's the one who actually *sees* them?"

"You've gotten used to it," Andrea said loftily. "The rest of us don't want to."

A bit of laughter rippled through the room and the tension eased, though the puppet on the table continued to stare at nothing with fixed white eyes.

"I'm just glad April is at her grandmother's today," Sally said. "She used to have nightmares about my puppets coming alive at night, and this . . . well, she can't see this."

"April's your daughter?" Melinda said.

Sally nodded. "She's excited about the old house, but now I'm starting to wonder."

"What's the next step?" Kevin swirled his empty glass. His posture became looser as the alcohol took effect. He had addressed the room in general, though the question was meant for Melinda—he clearly wasn't quite ready to address her directly about the ghost.

Melinda said, "We need to find out—" And abruptly everyone in the house was gone. Melinda was under the kitchen table on her hands and knees. The tile floor was the same, but it was cleaner, newer. So was the table, or what Melinda could see of it from underneath. A lace cloth hung over the edges, blurring the world beyond the table legs with woven mist. Melinda knelt on the hard floor, a china doll in her hands. It had black hair tied with red ribbons, a shiny white face, and painted blue eyes. Melinda recognized it as one of the dolls from the closet in the upstairs bedroom.

"Then they'll just have to move," said a male voice steeped in ice. "That's the whole point of a mortgage, isn't it? You can't pay it, you lose the house and land."

"But, sir," said another man, "the head of the household was called away to fight in the war. The family can't make the payments at the moment, not on a soldier's wages. When he comes back and returns to his job, he'll take them up again. Other banks are allowing—"

"I don't *care* about other banks," the first man said, and Melinda knew who it was in the way people know things in dreams. The man was her father, and his voice both fascinated and frightened her. Father made her stomach tight. He made her feel like a mouse. She crouched over her doll, hoping he wouldn't hear her.

"The man owes us money and he isn't paying," Father continued. "Draw up the foreclosure papers and get the family out. The farmland is prime, and I want it for other things."

"Sir, with respect, I feel I should tell you that people around town are starting to talk," the second man said. His voice wavered, but he plunged on. "This is the fourth soldier-run farm you've fore-closed on in two months. People are saying your actions are unpatriotic. Your reputation is being—"

A terrible crash shook the table. Melinda buried a frightened squeak into her doll's dress. She peeped out through the lace tablecloth and saw four trouser-clad legs all crushed together at the edge of the table. One of the men—Father—was shoving the other facedown onto the table. The wood above her creaked. Melinda's heart beat quick taps in her chest.

"Are you questioning my orders, Mr. Benson?" Father asked. His voice was perfectly calm, as if he were asking after Mr. Benson's wife or trying to decide whether the gardener should cut the grass a day early. "Are you?"

"N-no, sir," Mr. Benson gasped. His voice was muffled by the table. Melinda knew who the man was then. Mr. Benson was a nice man, almost sixty, with silver hair on his head and lollipops in his pockets. Now Father had him. Melinda's stomach hurt.

"I think you *are* questioning me," Father said. "I think you need a lesson in who is in charge around my house and my business."

Father's legs turned and walked toward one of the cupboards. Mr. Benson gave another gasp, this one of relief, as his legs straightened, but a moment later Father slammed something down on the table. Melinda jumped.

"Eat it," said Father conversationally.

"Sir," Mr. Benson quavered, "that's a can of dog food."

"I know what it is, Mr. Benson. Eat it or you'll be out on the street. I suspect at your age that might be difficult."

Melinda's guts churned. She hoped Mr. Benson would refuse. She hoped he would hit Father and walk out the door, straightening his suit coat as he went. But the thought was futile. No one said no to Father.

Mr. Benson hesitated for a long moment. "Sir . . . I . . ."

"Yes, Benson?"

"Sir . . . I'll need a spoon."

Melinda closed her eyes.

"Your fingers will suffice, I believe, Mr. Benson," Father said.

Another pause. "Of course, sir." The can scraped slightly as it left the tabletop and Melinda caught the wet, mealy smell of dog food. She heard the squashy sound of a pair of fingers digging into a damp mass and a choking noise as Mr. Benson did as Father ordered. Melinda felt horrible. She wished she could be anywhere else, even at the bottom of a well, and she hugged her doll tightly.

"That's enough, Mr. Benson," Father said at last. "Go take care of those papers, will you?"

"Yes, Mr. Ray." Mr. Benson's footsteps hurried from the kitchen, and Melinda heard the back door slam. Melinda stayed where she was, her heart still pounding. Father washed his hands in the sink, then walked past the table one more time. Abruptly, the lacy tablecloth was yanked upward and two hard hands seized Melinda. They pulled her out into the open.

"What do you think you're doing?" Father demanded. "Spying on me, are you?"

Melinda was too frightened to do anything but clutch her doll and stare at him. Father's black hair was slicked down with shiny pomade, and his angry brown eyes were hard as marble. His dark suit with its perfect pinstripes and flawless silk was the same he wore every day. His harsh hands gripped her sides and held her up as easily as she held her doll. Tears welled up in her eyes.

"No answer, eh? I'll teach you respect, young missy." He carried her to the cellar door. "I'll teach you to be a lady."

Melinda's voice broke free at this. "No, Father! Don't! That's where the monsters are!"

"Then maybe they'll teach you to be good." He opened the door. It gaped like a fish's mouth, and he yanked her halfway down the stone steps. No electric lights in the cellar—everyone used candles, but they were kept on a shelf out of Melinda's reach. Earthy darkness surrounded her as Father set her on the stairs. Fear paralyzed her. The darkness writhed and moved, breathing, waiting. She hugged her doll even tighter.

"None of that!" Father snapped, and snatched her doll away. She cried out and lunged for it, but he yanked it out of reach. Its head hit the stone wall and Melinda heard the *crack* of splintering china. She burst into tears.

"Now look what you did. You sit down here and think about what just happened, Florence. Maybe some time with the creatures that crawl through the dark will teach you something." With that, he stalked up the stairs and shut the door, plunging the cellar into darkness. Bereft of her doll and anyone who might help her, Melinda began to cry. Then a pair of hands reached out of the darkness and grabbed her shoulders with chilly strength. Melinda screamed.

7

"MELINDA!" THE VOICE was familiar. It cut through the screams. "Melinda, stop! Please! Melinda, can you hear me?"

Melinda blinked. She was in the kitchen again, but it was different. Older. Old. She was sitting at the table, not under it. Lights. It was light, not dark. She was sitting on a wooden chair, not stone steps. A man's face swam into her field of vision. Melinda gasped in fear, but it wasn't Father. It was someone else. Jim. Her husband.

Something snapped inside her head, and everything righted itself. She was sitting in Kevin and Sally's kitchen with a concerned group of people around her. Jim was holding her shoulders and looking into her face.

"I'm all right," she said. "It was . . . I had a vision, is all."

"A vision?" Sally asked. "What do you mean?"

"Do you want a drink?" Kevin asked. "You look like you could use one."

"Some tea, if you have it," Melinda said.

Kevin filled a kettle while Andrea, who looked relieved at having something to do, found a cup and a box of tea bags.

"What's a vision?" Sally asked again.

Melinda found she was having trouble concentrating. This vision had been much more intense than most, and it left her feeling scattered and drained. Jim stepped in. "Sometimes she gets impressions or even full-blown visions about things that have happened to people who died. It's like she experiences memories of ghosts, or even memories of a place or object."

"I've heard of that," Sally said. "It must be difficult if you have one when you're driving."

At that, Melinda gave a short bark of a laugh. "Completely true, unfortunately. Wow. Give me a minute, and I'll tell you what happened."

Eventually, tea was produced and Melinda drank, using the heat and spicy taste to ground herself in the here and now, to remind herself that she had a body that still worked. It was a trick she had learned from her grandmother. Eat something after a vision, her Grandma had said, whose preferred postvision treat had been oatmeal-raisin cookies and milk. Food keeps body and soul together.

Once she felt more herself again, she related what she had seen and felt as best she could.

"Making subordinates eat dog food?" Sally said. "Locking his daughter in the cellar? That's horrible!"

"Sounds like my great-great-grandfather Frederick was a real winner," Kevin said, folding his arms. "No wonder Grandma Florence had mental troubles. I want to go back in time and kick his ass."

"Do you think it's *his* ghost in the hallway?" Andrea said.

Melinda thought about that. "It's possible. He died before his time, and the hallway ghost is certainly angry about something. Frederick Ray seemed to be angry a lot, or he did in my vision. But . . ."

"But what?" Jim asked.

"He kept it very cool," Melinda said. "He never yelled that I saw. He was more like a knife made of ice. Not someone who would scream and howl like the hallway ghost does."

"Should we go up there and ask?" Kevin said. All traces of his earlier stubbornness had disappeared. "Seems the logical thing to do."

"I don't think I'm up to it today," Melinda said. "Actually, I think I want to go home."

"Of course, of course," Kevin said solicitously. "I wasn't thinking. Do you need help out to the car?"

"I can help her," Jim put in.

"No, I'm fine," Melinda said, rising. "It's just my psyche that's battered. Andrea, would you mind packing up and dropping the stuff we've cataloged back at the store? I'll love you forever."

Andrea clicked her laptop shut. "How can I turn that down?"

"Is it safe to stay in the house?" Sally asked as Melinda and Jim headed for the door.

"Should be," Melinda told her. "People have lived in this house with that ghost for a couple-three generations without a problem. The spirit apparently doesn't care what you do as long as you don't go down that hallway. So don't go down that hallway."

"We won't," Kevin said with feeling. He set Melinda's cup in the sink and brought her used tea bag over to the trash. Something in the wastebasket seemed to catch his eye and he bent to pluck it out, but Jim, his hand on Melinda's elbow, was already moving her out of the kitchen. Neither of them saw him stare at the little business card.

"Since when have you become a fainting flower?" Jim asked, setting the tray down on the coffee table. Two brimming cups of cocoa steamed on it beside a large bowl of popcorn.

Melinda shifted against the sofa pillows. "Since you offered to drive me home, make snacks, and give me a foot rub."

"I didn't say anything about a foot rub." Jim sat down next to her and grabbed a handful of popcorn. "Except maybe the one that you owe me."

"I owe *you*?"

"From the way I won Kevin over for you with the magic of male bonding. Don't think I didn't see the 'treats for later' look you gave me."

"Oh. Right. That." She looked at him with heavy-lidded eyes, made a sultry moue, and dropped her voice into a husky register. "Are you sure a foot rub is the kind of treat you want?"

In answer, Jim kicked off his shoes and put his feet into Melinda's lap. "Yep."

"Oh, come *on*! I had a vision today!"

"Aren't you the one who's always saying that you need to ground yourself after a vision?" Jim countered. "I can't think of anything more grounding than a foot rub." He wiggled his toes at her.

"I meant for me, you fool!"

Jim made an enormously overdone put-upon face. "All right, all right. If you must, we can both be happy." With a bit of shifting, they managed to arrange themselves on the wide couch so they both had their bare feet in each other's laps, or more accurately, on each other's chests. Jim's feet were warm in Melinda's hands. She resisted the urge to play "This Little Piggy," partly because Jim held her own feet hostage and partly because she wasn't sure if the idea was a leftover from her recent time inside the head of a little girl. Jim's gentle fingers worked her toes and soles, and Melinda sighed and felt herself begin to relax.

"You realize," Jim said, "that since this is reciprocal, it means we're still on for more treats later."

"Is that all you're going to think about?"

"As I recall," Jim said blandly, "*you* brought it up first."

"So I did. Pass me the popcorn."

At that point, Melinda's cell phone rang from the coffee table. Jim made a "forget it" gesture, but from the couch Melinda could see the caller ID on the screen. It was Andrea.

"Might be important," she said, disentangling herself and reaching for it. Jim sat up and consoled himself by taking up a cup of cooling cocoa.

"I hope I'm not interrupting something important," Andrea said. "Actually, since I'm insanely jealous of your love life, I hope I did interrupt. At least a little."

"What's going on?" Melinda asked. She was already missing the feeling of Jim's hands caressing her feet. "Did you find more information about the Ray house?"

"Nope. That I would have e-mailed to you. I have a problem. One of those . . . *special* problems."

Melinda came quietly alert. "Is there something wrong at the store or your apartment?"

"Sort of the second one. Look, this would be easier to talk about in person. Could you meet us at Village Java downtown?"

"Us?"

"It's not actually my problem."

Melinda folded her phone and looked at Jim. He eyed her over his cup. "Why do I have the feeling there's going to be a rain check on the treats?"

"More like a thunderstorm check, but yeah. I'll try to be quick."

"Do you want me to go with you?" he asked, annoyance shifting to concern.

"No, thanks. But if things go south, I promise to shout for help like a good fainting flower."

A few minutes later, Andrea was waving at her from a corner table at Village Java. Sitting with her at the tiny table was an elderly Asian woman Melinda didn't recognize. Her silver hair was braided and bunned, and she wore a red pantsuit. The knitting needles in her hands battled over a hank of yarn like soldiers willing to die for several hundred feet of pink wool. Melinda pulled out a chair and sat down, inhaling the heavy scent of coffee. The latte machine behind the counter hissed like someone was throttling an anaconda. The old woman didn't even pause in her knitting, though she did look up as Andrea greeted Melinda.

"This is Mrs. Xing," Andrea said, pronouncing the name *Shing,* and the old lady nodded. "She's my landlady."

"Nice to meet you," Melinda said politely.

"You ghost lady?" Mrs. Xing asked.

Straightforward. There seemed to be a lot of that going around today. "That's me," she said. "What's going on?"

"Mrs. Xing's husband passed away a few days ago," Andrea explained.

"Oh, I'm so sorry," Melinda said.

"You not be sorry," Mrs. Xing said. "I not sorry. Bad, bad man. Make life miserable for everyone. I glad he gone. My son, too."

"Your son is gone, too?" Melinda said, trying to keep up.

Mrs. Xing snorted. "My son not gone. My son a big lawyer for a big company." A note of pride entered Mrs. Xing's voice. "His name Timmy. Timmy Xing. Maybe you heard of him?"

"I . . . I don't know many lawyers," Melinda said.

"Your marriage—it happy?"

"What? Yes!"

"Damn." Another pink row of stitches flashed from the needles. "You ever leave your husband, you call my Timmy, you got that? He going to have a lucky marriage, and it good luck if he marry a ghost lady. Very good."

"I'll remember that," Melinda said while Andrea hid a smile. "Exactly what can I help you with, Mrs. Xing?"

"Don't rush old lady." More pink yarn wove itself beneath her stabbing silver needles. "First you listen. Mr. Xing very smart man. One day after we married, he decide to leave Hong Kong very fast, very very fast. We come to America and start new life. He even give us new names—Mr. and Mrs. Xing instead of Mr. and Mrs. Wang. This because in America, Wang is very rude name, he say. He find way to buy apartment building. He charge high rent in good part of town, very smart. But we never have any money. Why? Because, he say, we have taxes and things to fix and the building loan. We eat boiled rice with sugar every day for breakfast because that is all we can afford. I learn to cut coupons and never buy anything unless it on sale. I don't have television because it take up too much electricity. I make clothes for me and for Timmy. I knit many things and sell them. But Mr. Xing say we still in debt, we never have enough. Other kids laugh at Timmy because of his home-made clothes, and we never celebrate holidays or birthdays because we have no extra money. Our apartment always cold in winter. Mr. Xing say only reason we not living on the street is that we have building. Timmy want to go to law school, but there is no money for the good school he wants, and government say he can't have scholarships, so he take many, many loans and goes to not-so-good school. Thousands of dollars in debt for third-best school, even though Timmy so smart, would be A student at top school. I stay home and keep working so I can try to send him at least a little money, but there almost never anything to send."

"It sounds awful," Melinda said. "What was Mr. Xing doing all day?"

"Taking care of building. That was what he tell me. Or he have to go away to talk to zoning people or to tax people or to contractors. Very, very busy all the time. And then two days ago, *pwah!* Mr. Xing die. Heart attack. I very upset. My husband for twenty-eight years—gone! I thought I loved him, and I feel very sad. And I wonder, how will I live with so much debt? Timmy has starter job, lives in tiny apartment. Barely able to pay rent because student loans so high. He can't support old mother yet. I will lose building. I will lose my home and eat out of garbage cans."

Melinda felt sick. "That's terrible. What are you going to do?"

"Nothing."

"Nothing?" Melinda echoed. "I don't understand."

"Oh, you'll love this," Andrea said, arms folded.

"I was cleaning apartment because I needed something to do and because people would be coming after funeral—and how would I pay for that, I wonder? Mr. Xing had big desk, and I was forbidden to touch it, but it needed dusting, so I dust it, and then I decide to open a drawer to see what inside. You know what I find?"

"I have no idea," Melinda said, though she was privately guessing. Her first guess was some sort of diary with shocking secrets hidden inside, ones that Mr. Xing didn't want made public. Maybe that was why his ghost was hanging around—he wanted his wife's assurance that she would keep quiet, or he wanted her to burn the diary, or he wanted her forgiveness for whatever it was he had done. The last possibility was the most common and unfortunately the hardest to arrange. Granting forgiveness was easier said than done, and it got worse after someone had died and was forced to plead their case through an interpreter. But Melinda would do it. If not her, who?

"I go through drawer," Mrs. Xing said, "and I find life insurance policy for two million dollars. Still in force. I millionaire now."

"Oh!" Melinda shifted mental gears from sympathy into cautious cheer. "Well, that's a piece of good news, then, isn't it? Even though Mr. Xing died?" Then something occurred to her. "Wait. You said you thought you loved your husband and you were sad when he died. But you also said he's a bad man and you're *not* sorry he's dead. What—?"

"I find more." Mrs. Xing's needles flickered and flashed, tiny swords over a pink field. "I find bank statement that say Mr. Xing have three million dollars in account with his name only. I find deeds to four more apartment buildings in other cities. I find stock portfolio worth almost seven million. I find second life insurance policy worth two more million."

Melinda stared, struck speechless at this revelation. Andrea nodded. Melinda couldn't imagine. What sort of man would force his wife and son to live in poverty while he sat on millions of dollars?

"Mr. Xing leave will," Mrs. Xing continued. "Everything except life insurance money go to Timmy, but Timmy promise to give much more to me. We both have lots of money now. But my love for Mr. Xing turn into hate. I work and work my entire life and give my money to Mr. Xing. He make us think we must eat plain boiled rice and sleep in cold rooms in tiny apartment when we could live in nice house and wear good clothes and send our son to best school in country. Bad, bad man. You see this?" She held up her knitting. When Melinda and Andrea nodded, she said, "Mr. Xing hate pink. I knit this sweater for him to wear in his coffin. I also buy cheapest casket they have. It look like cardboard, and everyone at his funeral can laugh at him in his pink sweater and his cheap casket. I bury him and I spit on his grave. Then I fly to Tahiti."

"Good for you," Andrea said. "You deserve it."

"But you still have a problem," Melinda prompted.

"Mr. Xing not gone from apartment," Mrs. Xing explained. "He still there. I know it. I hear his voice, just a little, but I can't understand what he saying. Timmy hear it, too. He staying with me until funeral over."

"Timmy or Mr. Xing?" Andrea asked.

Mrs. Xing gave her a hard look over her embattled knitting needles, then turned to Melinda. "I tell Andrea about problem, and she tell me you can help, so we call. You help me, ghost lady?"

"Of course," Melinda said. "Do you want to talk to him now? We can try it."

Without a word, Mrs. Xing stuffed her knitting into a bag and swept out of the coffee shop. Andrea and Melinda hurried to catch up. They trotted across the night-darkened square to Andrea's apartment building, a tall structure made with brick by an unimaginative architect. Mrs. Xing unlocked the front door with her key and led them into the basement, where she unlocked another door.

"I already looking for nice condo," she said. "I never want to look at this place again."

"You know," Andrea said, "fun as this will probably be, my role in this is over, and I have the feeling I'll just be in the way. Why don't I just disappear like a good assistant? Melinda, I'll see you tomorrow. Mrs. Xing, I hope everything works out. You're in good hands." And she vanished up the stairs.

"She good girl," Mrs. Xing said. "Always pay her rent on time. Too bad she never get married."

Melinda cocked her head. "What do you mean?"

"That my talent." Mrs. Xing put her key away. "You see ghosts, I see marriages. You sit down in coffee shop, I already know you married, remember? And I know my Timmy have lucky marriage one day. But that Andrea—she die single lady. Too bad for her."

"So why did you marry Mr. Xing?" Melinda couldn't help asking.

"I see a marriage with Mr. Xing give me a son and lots of money. In China, this very lucky, very good. For my whole life, I think something wrong with my talent. I get son but not money. Now I know why."

Mrs. Xing swung the door open, revealing a stark, cramped apartment beyond. A single living area served as kitchen, living room, and dining room. Small windows set high in the walls would let in only miserly sunlight during the day. The furniture was thirdhand, minimal, and much repaired. The appliances in the tiny kitchen hadn't been updated since the seventies, and the cheap table looked like it might fall over if it supported much more than a small sandwich. The bulbs in all the fixtures threw grudging light, and Melinda guessed several were only forty watts. An ancient sewing machine sat in one corner. No television in evidence, or even a radio. The floors were scarred bare wood, and the beige walls looked tired. A short hallway led down toward what Melinda assumed were tiny bedrooms. Everything was as clean as bleach and elbow grease could get it, but the entire place felt tired. A simple coat of bright paint on the walls would have helped immeasurably. Melinda tried to imagine living in such a dreary place for more than twenty years and shuddered.

Mrs. Xing dropped her knitting bag on the trembling table and faced Melinda. "Well? You see him?"

Melinda looked around. "Not yet. Give it a minute."

A door opened and closed down the hallway. "Ma? That you?"

An Asian man in his late twenties emerged from the hall. He wore jeans, a green polo shirt, and running shoes. He had a whipcord build that bordered on thin, and Melinda wondered if his childhood eating situation was to blame. "I found two more bank statements in Dad's desk. And I think I've solved the—oh! I didn't know you'd brought people home."

"This my son, Timmy," Mrs. Xing said, and made introductions. "Melinda see ghosts. She going to help with Dad."

A startled look crossed Timmy's face. "You told . . . I mean . . . oh. That's . . . unexpected."

Melinda put on her most disarming smile. She'd been through this a thousand times. Whenever you can, Grandma often said, let the living know you sympathize with what they're going through. It makes a strange situation easier. And she was right. "I can understand. Your whole world's been turned upside down by what happened with your dad, and now on top of it all, I'm here telling you I can see ghosts. It must be a shock."

"It's not that," Timmy said. "It's just that I've already taken care of it."

It was Melinda's turn to look startled. "You have? How did—?"

A second Asian man appeared behind Mrs. Xing. He was an older version of Timmy, dressed in a battered jacket and ancient tie. His expression was distilled terror, and his fear spilled over into Melinda. Her stomach tightened and her heart sped up. He howled something in Chinese and tried to grab at Mrs. Xing, but his hands passed right through her. She turned slightly, as if vaguely aware of a faint breeze.

"He's here," Melinda said, quickly dropping into ghost lady mode. "Mrs. Xing, your husband is here, and he's very frightened. But he's speaking Chinese and I don't understand him."

"Speak English, you old fool," Mrs. Xing said to the empty air. Like most people in her situation, she didn't quite face the spot where the spirit was standing. "Why you make us live like poor trash when we could live like rich family, with high status and good life? Why you make your son hang his head in shame when he could be proud of his family? *Why?*"

"*Stop! STOP HER!*"

It took Melinda a moment to realize that Mr. Xing was talking not to his wife, but directly to Melinda. Unlike his wife, he had no accent. His fear hung thick in the air, tightening Melinda's throat. "Stop who?" she asked. "What's wrong? What's frightening you?"

"I don't understand this," Timmy put in. "Do you work for the other woman?"

A cold hand ran down Melinda's spine. "Other woman? What other woman?"

Mr. Xing vanished and popped back into existence right in front of Melinda. She jumped back with a start. The air temperature dropped ten degrees, and all the lights flickered. "*Ghost lady! It hurts! You have to stop her!*"

"You don't know her?" Timmy said.

"Know who?" Melinda demanded. One of the lightbulbs in the kitchen popped.

"Stop her, ghost lady! Please!"

"Wendy King." Timmy pointed. "She's in the bedroom where Dad had his desk."

Without a word, Melinda ran down the short hall and flung the door open. In a single glance she took in the little room inside—double bed, single nightstand, closet door, braided rug. The room was dominated by a large rolltop desk with lockable drawers. Despite the overall paucity of the furniture, the room was crowded because of the desk. It was in the way. Anyone who used this room would constantly be tripping over it or having to edge around it. It bespoke an owner who had decided his stuff was more important than anyone else's.

At the moment, the top of the desk was covered with lit candles. An all-too-familiar skull sat among them beside a brass bowl and a silver incense burner. Beside the desk stood Wendy King in her perfect gray suit. In one hand she held her gleaming silver knife. In the other she held a barbecue lighter. She was using it to light the incense. Tiny curls of green light crawled around the edges of the desk as she worked, and Melinda wondered if Wendy was able to see them. There was no sign of the spirit of Wendy's father.

Wendy looked up as Melinda burst in. A resigned look crossed her face. "Not you," she said. "Can't you just leave me alone to do my job?"

"You're terrifying Mr. Xing," Melinda said. "You have to stop this. It'll tear him apart."

"So you say." Wendy took a firmer hold on the knife and took a deep breath. "And what does it matter? He's dead and shouldn't be here. He tortured his family their entire lives, and now he's torturing them after his death. You're the one standing in the way of their peace, Melinda. What gives you that right?"

"Whatever Mr. Xing did, he doesn't deserve to be tortured," Melinda said. Her mind raced, trying to think of something to say or do to stop Wendy. Unfortunately, the only thing that came to mind was physical force, and that would only end badly for everyone. For one thing, Wendy could press charges, and while Melinda had no compunctions about striking out in the defense of another person, it would be impossible to explain the circumstances to the police. And, she had to admit, she didn't really know how. Maybe she could break the skull on the desk, bring a halt to Wendy's ritual. But that would still be property damage.

"I want him gone," snarled Timmy as he entered the bedroom. "The man was a bastard. Did my mother tell you what he did to us? How he made us live in poverty while he made millions? I just found two more bank statements in that goddamn desk, both with accounts totaling over two *more* million dollars. I went to school hungry, and I wore a thin jacket all winter because my ass-hole of a father was too cheap to buy me a warm coat. I never had a birthday cake because Dad said it was a waste of money we didn't have. You see this?" He pulled aside his collar to bare one shoulder. An ugly pink scar puckered the skin and traveled down part of his chest. "When I was fifteen, I was riding a friend's skateboard and I fell against a wrought-iron fence. I cut myself really bad, but my dad wouldn't take me to the hospital for stitches because it would cost too much. Ma bandaged me up as best she could, but it left me with an ugly bunch of scars. If you can get rid of Dad, Wendy, do it. And if it hurts, I'll give you a bonus."

Mr. Xing appeared next to his son. His silver hair was wild, and his wrinkled face contorted with fear and pain. *"No! You don't understand! You have to stop her!"*

But Timmy stomped out of the room. Mr. Xing shot Melinda a pleading glance and vanished again. The cloying, nauseating smell of incense began to fill the room and more green light crawled around the desk. It seemed to hiss softly, like a nest of snakes.

"You see?" Wendy said. "Not only do I have Timmy Xing's permission, I have his blessing. Now . . . if you don't mind? Or perhaps I should call Mr. Xing the younger in here so he can escort you away?"

Melinda ground her teeth. Wendy's solution was the wrong way to handle this. Every instinct she had told her so. But there seemed to be nothing Melinda could do. Ignoring Melinda, Wendy opened a book on the bed and tapped the bowl with a striker. The bell-like sound rang through the room. Mr. Xing appeared at once and screamed, his face twisted and distorted like a bunched-up pillow. Pain thundered over Melinda. She put her hands over her ears and fled the room as Wendy struck the bowl again and Mr. Xing screamed.

She found Timmy Xing engaged in heated discussion with his mother in the kitchen. Mrs. Xing was sitting at the kitchen table, her embattled knitting needles once again busy in her lap.

"Why you bring this other ghost lady woman here?" Mrs. Xing was saying. "I tell you I find someone already."

"She just knocked on the door, Ma," Timmy said. "She said the spirits led her here. I thought you'd sent her or something. As long as she gets rid of Dad, who cares?"

Mr. Xing popped into existence behind Timmy. He was clawing at the air, trying to get his son's attention, but Timmy couldn't hear or see him. In the bedroom, the bowl rang a third time and Mr. Xing screamed. Terror ripped at Melinda's nerves and she had to steel herself against it in order to function.

"Listen," Melinda said, forcing her voice to remain steady, "we don't have much time. Wendy King is a . . . a sort of medium. She forces spirits to cross over into the next world. It's painful and terrifying beyond anything we can imagine."

Timmy folded his arms. "Good."

"You can't mean that," Melinda said.

"Yes, I can."

"Look, your dad did terrible things to you. You have him in your power now just as he had you in his power for so long. Do you want to be as terrible as he was?"

"Why should I care?" Timmy countered. "I suffered all my life. Let him suffer for a few minutes."

A muffled chanting came from the other room and a trickle of incense smoke reached Melinda's nostrils. Mr. Xing begged Melinda with his eyes. Inspiration struck.

"Once he's gone, you'll never know the answer," she said. "You'll never know why he did it."

"So?" Timmy said. "What difference would it make if I knew?"

"I want to know." Mrs. Xing's knitting needles never slowed. "I want to know very much."

"Then stop her," Melinda said, "and let me talk to him. I can find out for you."

Timmy looked at his mother, then tightened his arms across his chest. "Is he here?" At Melinda's nod, he added, "Then tell him to talk fast."

Another form appeared in the room—the blurry ghost with the fringe of beard and receding hairline. Wendy King's father and spirit guide. He approached Mr. Xing, who cowered in fear, and stretched out his hand. A shining silver thread appeared in the air. It ran from Mr. Xing's chest and disappeared into the bedroom where Wendy was working. Wendy's father solemnly laid his hand on the thread. Mr. Xing flinched, and Melinda felt his revulsion, his violation. The other spirit was touching something intensely personal. It was like being groped by a stranger who had dipped his hands in sewer water. Wendy's father paced along the thread, slowly following it back to the bedroom, where Wendy waited with her silver knife.

"Why did you do it?" Melinda asked Mr. Xing. "Quick! We don't have much time. Is that why you're still here? Did you want to tell them that?"

"I'm . . . I can't . . ." Mr. Xing gasped. He was doubled over, clutching his stomach.

Melinda knelt next to him, aware of how strange it must look to Timmy and Mrs. Xing. "You have to try," she urged. "You can do it. Let me help you. Why didn't you tell your family about the money?"

Wendy's father had reached the hall. Mr. Xing unbent partway. Wendy's father was no longer in sight, but the silver thread hung in the air, connecting Mr. Xing to his desk in the room beyond.

Melinda felt that connection somehow, though she couldn't have explained it. She also didn't know how long Wendy's ritual would take, but she had a terrible feeling it wouldn't take overly long.

"*Tell them I did it for them,*" Mr. Xing said. "*I wanted to protect them!*"

"He says he did it to protect you," Melinda said.

"From what?" Timmy scoffed.

"*Shè huì hěi,*" Mr. Xing said, then gasped as another wave of pain washed over him. "*Shè huì hěi.*"

"He's saying a word in Chinese," Melinda said. She struggled to repeat it.

"It means nothing to me," Timmy said.

Mrs. Xing stopped knitting.

Both Timmy and Melinda stared at her motionless hands. It was the first time Melinda had seen her not working except when she was on her feet, and judging by the expression on Timmy's face, it was a first for him, too.

"*Shè huì hěi.* It mean *black society*," Mrs. Xing said in a soft voice. "Hong Kong mafia. You borrow money from them, old fool?"

"*Stole it,*" Mr. Xing said. "*I never told my wife, but just after we were married in Hong Kong, I lost my job. I was ashamed that I couldn't find work, so I didn't tell her. Instead, I started to run drug money for a local Shè huì hěi lord in Hong Kong. One day, I just ran with the money I was supposed to deliver.*"

That was why we left Hong Kong so fast and why I changed our names. I ran all the way to America, to Grandview, far away from the black society. I bought this building, but then I became afraid the society would find me. I was afraid they would come for me and for my family. So I hid myself as a poor man. A rich man is easy to find, but no one finds a poor man. It didn't help. I was always scared they were coming for me. I was sure that if I spent anything, if I called attention to myself, they would know. I was terrified every minute I was alive. And now I'm dead. I'm so sorry. Timmy, Ming-Mei, I'm sorry."

Melinda quickly relayed this. Looks of shock and amazement played over the faces of Timmy and Mrs. Xing.

"Why can't he leave?" Timmy asked. He seemed less certain, but his arms were still crossed.

"I need to know you're safe," Mr. Xing said. The silver thread vibrated heavily like an old guitar string. Mr. Xing screamed again. Melinda clapped her hands over her ears, but the scream still tore through her head like dull scissors through paper. Through Mr. Xing, she could feel Wendy's cold fingers questing for the thread. They touched it, lost it, found it again.

"Stop!" Melinda cried. "Stop! I can't help unless you stop screaming!"

Mr. Xing staggered, then forced back the screams. He gasped, *"In my desk is a yellow card.*

From China. It has a Hong Kong address . . . on it. Send my death certificate . . . anonymously."

"So they'll know you're dead," Melinda said, "and won't come after you or hurt your family."

"No reason . . . to hurt them . . . if the thief is dead." Mr. Xing gasped.

Melinda gave the information to Timmy and Mrs. Xing. "Will you do that? It's his last request."

Mr. Xing twisted inhumanly and the howl of terror that escaped him nearly broke Melinda's eardrums. The aging table collapsed into kindling and the kitchen faucet burst, sending water spouting into the air. Mrs. Xing was left in her kitchen chair, staring at the pile of broken wood, her pink knitting still in her lap. Timmy firmed his jaw. In the other room, Melinda could feel Wendy raising her knife, the spirit of her father guiding her hand.

"Please!" Melinda said. "Will you do it?"

There was a tiny pause. Rusty water continued to gush in the kitchen. "All right," said Timmy. "I'll do it, Dad."

Mr. Xing stopped screaming and turned his head. The thread vibrated like a harp string. *"That light,"* he said. *"It's . . . beautiful."*

"Go!" Melinda said. "Quick!"

"Is it for me? I . . . I think it's . . . it's . . . oh!" The thread vanished, and so did Mr. Xing. The room felt as empty as a cave.

Several busy moments followed. Timmy got under the sink and shut the water valve off. Melinda got a mop. Mrs. Xing watched from her chair near the shattered table.

"What happened?" Timmy asked at last. "Is he gone?"

"He is," Melinda said uncertainly, "but I can't tell—"

"He's gone." Wendy entered the room, duffel bag in her hand. "My spirit guide and I cut his ties to this world, showed him the way to the next."

"Was it you," Mrs. Xing said, then pointed to Melinda, "or you?"

"It was me," said Wendy. "Definitely. I felt the thread cut."

It flashed through Melinda's head to lie, to tell Timmy and Mrs. Xing that Mr. Xing had crossed over painlessly and happily, but she almost as quickly discarded the idea. They had lived through enough lies. Melinda herself felt torn. Had Mr. Xing crossed over before Wendy's knife had struck? She had no way of knowing. Resentment for Wendy gathered inside her like a poisoned bloom.

"I'm not so sure," Melinda said. "I saw him go right at the moment the thread vanished, but . . . I can't tell for certain. If he felt pain, it was very short."

"Still acting the child, aren't you?" Wendy said in a motherly tone that set Melinda's teeth on edge.

She felt like Cinderella, mop in hand, facing her cool, calm stepmother dressed in gray. "You really need to learn to take responsibility for your own work, Melinda, and understand that you can't always have it your own way."

"Take responsibility?" Melinda repeated. Her temper rose, and she set the mop carefully aside. "What is that supposed to mean?"

"When you get more experienced, maybe you'll understand."

"Fight between ghost ladies," said Mrs. Xing from her chair. "Very bad luck for everyone. Gray ghost lady—you not married?"

The question seemed to throw Wendy, and Melinda allowed herself a moment of mean gladness. "Why . . . no, I'm not."

"And you won't ever be. I can see that. Too bad. Lots of good luck—wasted." She got up and dropped her pink knitting into the kitchen trash. "Thank you for getting rid of Mr. Xing. You go now. I have to plan trip to Tahiti."

"I believe you mentioned a bonus, Mr. Xing?" Wendy said.

"Yeah, I did mention it. Thanks for your help." Timmy ushered both women firmly into the hall. "Thanks again." And he shut the door.

8

MELINDA ROUNDED ON Wendy in the dingy basement hallway. Smells of damp and mold swirled around her. "You're unbelievable," she said. "Do you always walk around with your hand out like a bellboy in a bad hotel?"

"The man just became a multimillionaire," Wendy said. "He could afford some extra. I'm a little mystified, to tell the truth. Poor people who become rich are usually more generous."

The anger blossomed and burst, filling Melinda with red rage. She leaned into Wendy's face. "You need to leave Grandview," Melinda hissed. "I want you out of this town. I want you to leave people alone and stop hurting spirits with your bag of tricks."

"And here I was, ready to extend you a business proposal," Wendy said.

This was the last thing Melinda had been expecting to hear. The offer derailed Melinda, and she floundered for a response. "B-business . . . proposal?"

"Of course. No reason we can't be civil. We can divide Grandview in half. I'll take the west end, and you take the east. Or the reverse, if you'd prefer. Main Street can be the dividing line. It's simple and elegant and fair. You stay in your half, and I'll stay in mine. Deal?"

Once again, Melinda was struck speechless. For a long moment, she could do nothing but stare at Wendy in disbelief. Then her voice came back and seemed to speak of its own volition. "What if a spirit crosses the boundary? What if a spirit from your side of town comes to me for help?"

"Then you just call me," Wendy said reasonably. "Just as I'll call you if the reverse happens."

Freaking unlikely, Melinda thought. "No. No deals. No way."

Wendy shrugged. "Your loss. But I'll tell you something, Melinda—you can't get rid of me. I'm here to stay. Grandview needs me. You've been bumbling along, letting these ghosts stay behind with their petty complaints and sapping energy from the living when they should be moving into the Light. I'm stronger than you are, and more effective. Really, it would be in Grandview's best interest if you concentrated on running your quaint little shop for the tourists."

As Wendy spoke, the figure of her father's spirit bloomed into existence behind her. His bearded face was still too blurry to make out many features. The air took on a chill.

Melinda bit back more outrage. "Wendy, Grandview needs you to stop," she pleaded instead. "Did you even try to find out what was going on with the Xing family?"

"Timmy told me everything. Mr. Xing was a horrible man who forced his family to live in poverty while he sat on a pile of money," Wendy said. "What else was there to know?"

"But there was more to it than that," Melinda said. "Mrs. Xing—and then Timmy—wanted to know why he did it. It turned out Mr. Xing was on the run from Hong Kong gangsters. He was afraid that living like a rich man would call attention to himself and his family. He couldn't let himself enjoy his money because he was afraid all the time. It wasn't a good solution, no, but at least now Timmy and Mrs. Xing know what happened and why, and that gives them some resolution, some peace. Did you try to find any of that out before you pulled out that silver knife?"

Wendy hesistated, and a flicker of doubt crossed her face. "How did you learn this?"

"By *listening*. Mr. Xing's spirit told me everything, and once he did, he was able to cross into the Light. At least, I think he did. You might have cut him away first. I couldn't tell." Melinda flicked a glance at the blurry ghost. "Can't you hear them speaking? Can't you feel their pain?"

Wendy hesitated again, and Melinda pressed her advantage. "Look," she said, "I could show you how it *really* works, how to cross ghosts over without hurting them. You have some awareness of the spirit world, but you have no empathy. These spirits have feelings, they have needs. What you do to them is cruel. I could help you to see that. Let me help you. Please."

Wendy seemed to be thinking, and Melinda held her breath. Then the spirit leaned down and whispered in Wendy's ear. The words were soft and rapid. Wendy's face hardened.

"You're jealous," Wendy said. "You're weak. It takes you a long time to deal with a spirit. I'm strong. Strong and efficient. A pity. We would have made a good team."

With that, she strode quickly up the basement stairs and away.

"Why can't I be a man?" Melinda raged as she slammed the door.

Jim poked his head into the foyer. "It would make our marriage awkward, for one thing," he said. "And your clothes wouldn't fit. Why do you want to be a man?"

"Then I could just punch her lights out or get her drunk or steal her distributor cap or something." Melinda flung her jacket over the bannister, stormed past Jim into the living room, and flung herself down onto the sofa. The anger pushed her, shoved her around like a wild steam valve, and the words just spewed out of her. "Can you steal her distributor cap? I don't even know what that is, but it sounds like it would do something horrible to her car."

"It would," said Jim uncertainly from the doorway. "Who are we talking about here? Andrea? Your mother?"

Melinda rounded on him like a dragon. "No! Who have I been upset about for the last two days?"

"Oh, no, you don't." Jim put up his hands. "I'm not falling for the guessing game trap. Who are you yelling about so I know who to commiserate on?"

"Wendy King."

"Ah." Jim paused. "Okay, I'm at a loss here. Do you want me to offer solutions or listen while you vent?"

"I don't know." Melinda folded her arms across her chest. She felt ready to bite something. She could chew through steel. The thought of Wendy loose, slashing and slicing her way through the spirit world—deliberately causing pain and suffering even now that she knew better—incensed Melinda. It was the worst form of bullying, and

Melinda loathed bullies. "I'm ready to kill her and then not help her cross over."

"You don't mean that." Jim edged up behind the couch and put careful hands on Melinda's shoulders. Melinda almost batted his hands away and caught herself just in time. She wasn't mad at Jim, and spewing anger all over him wouldn't help her or her situation.

"I don't know what I mean anymore," she said. "I'm angry and I'm scared and I don't know what to do."

"I don't think boosting her distributor cap is a step in the right direction," Jim said, massaging gently. Melinda closed her eyes and let him work. "Tell the truth, I don't know what your options are. You can't force her out of town. It sounds like you can't convince her to stop."

"Not in this lifetime," Melinda growled.

"Which, in your case, means more than for most people."

"Every time I talk to that woman, her father's spirit interferes," Melinda continued. "I don't know what he says or does, but Wendy never listens to reason when he's around, and he's *always* around. I want to punch him, too. How do you handle it?"

"Handle what?"

"Wanting to punch someone. Isn't that the usual guy thing?"

"You mean women never want to fight?"

"Not as often as men do."

"Says who?"

"Says everyone."

Jim kept up the gentle kneading. "Sounds like the woman in the room is more pugnacious than the man right now."

A retort rose, but Melinda forced it back with a deep breath. "Yeah, you're right. This is just—I don't know how to handle it, and it's freaking me out."

"I can think of at least seven ways to unfreak you," Jim said. "For tonight, anyway. And only three of them involve sex."

His fingers continued their work. "Do tell," Melinda said at last.

"I prefer to show."

In the morning, Melinda opened up the antique store as usual. Her mood was slightly better thanks to Jim's late-night ministrations—numbers two, three, and seven, specifically—but she still felt off-balance. At any moment, Wendy might come across another hapless spirit and torture it again. And the problem of the ghost in the Ray house hallway weighed on her mind. Melinda still couldn't figure out exactly who the spirit was or what it needed to move on, and the lack tugged at her, like an itch in a place she couldn't quite reach.

Fortunately, the morning remained busy. A fair number of customers came through the shop, not all of them buy-nothing browsers, and Melinda sold several pieces from Kevin Ray's house. She was recording them on the computer when Andrea came in, bearing a tall Styrofoam mug from Village Java.

"I have news," she said. "It's about the Ray family."

"Good news or bad news?"

"I-know-more-than-you-do news." Andrea sipped from her coffee mug. "Want to hear it?"

"Always."

"I heard from the historical society again, see, but this time the information comes from a sideways descendant. You know—a descendant of a Ray cousin instead of someone from the direct line?"

"Okay."

"This is more in the line of family gossip than actual historical fact," Andrea continued. "So it's less trustworthy, you understand."

Melinda leaned on the counter, intrigued and interested. "Gossip can be good. Tell!"

"All right. See, this descendant of the Ray cousin says that Frederick Ray—"

At that moment, the door opened, setting the customer bell to ringing merrily. Into the shop stampeded a small crowd of pantsuited women, all of them over fifty, all of them Asian.

"You Melinda Gordon?" one of the women asked. The others spread about around the shop, peering at the merchandise and chattering to one another in a mixture of Chinese and English.

"That's me," Melinda said without missing a beat.

"Mrs. Xing say this very good place to shop for antiques," one of the women said. "She say you have best antiques in state."

"We would never disagree with someone as wise as Mrs. Xing," Andrea said.

"How much?" said another woman, holding up a lace doily.

And it was more than two hours before Melinda and Andrea had the shop to themselves again.

"You were saying?" Melinda asked as they surveyed the store. It was devastated. Shelves were out of order. Clothes hung halfway off racks. Dolls sat askew. Toys were tipped over. The usual post-rush mess that would take more than an hour to straighten out. On the other hand, the cash register was full. Always a plus.

"I was saying about what?" Andrea straightened a set of windup clocks on their shelf, then turned to a rack of vintage dresses.

"The Ray cousin! What did you find out?"

"Ah. Him." Andrea secured a red silk dress on its puffy hanger. "You found out in your vision that Freddy Ray wasn't a very nice man."

"No kidding."

"He was less than non-nicer than you didn't not know."

Melinda tried to untangle that in her head and failed. "Explain."

"Frederick Ray was a land baron of the worst kind and definitely not a family man. That incident you saw in your vision? Apparently, he used to do that a lot. Locking Florence—and Arthur—in the cellar with no lights was a standard punishment for him. The cousin's family said that Frederick liked to tell people that *things* lived down there, too, and all the kids in the family were scared to set foot on the stairs. Another favorite was to shove the kids into a closet and lock it."

"Just goes to show that good money doesn't make a good father," Melinda said. "I wonder how many times he locked up Grandma Florence."

"Don't forget Arthur," Andrea pointed out, and Melinda remembered the closet door that had burst open and slapped her in the face. "While I can't imagine there's a parent alive who hasn't thought about locking their little darlings in a dark room for a few hours, I'd like to think the majority don't actually follow through."

"And it's likely the abuse didn't stop there," Melinda mused. "God. I'll bet it all has something to do with why Grandma Florence never left the house."

"Most likely." Andrea had finished with the dresses and was resetting a display of carved animals. Melinda, who was entering sales into the computer, noted idly that they were the animals from the Noah's ark set they had found in the Ray house. "But Frederick's abuse bled into the community. In your vision thing you overheard him abuse his clerk or whoever that was, and you heard him talk about throwing those people off their land."

"Yeah."

"That was common with Frederick Ray. He bought mortgages just to foreclose on them. He tricked farmers into thinking their land was poisoned so he could buy it for pennies. A couple of times Frederick acquired land because the original owner died rather suddenly and Frederick was able to buy everything at auction. Everyone in Grandview was afraid to bid against him, so he got hundreds of acres on the cheap."

Melinda stared. "Did Frederick kill the original owners to get their land?"

"Rumor only," Andrea said. "But you saw firsthand—or whatever hand a vision gives you— how he treated his employees and his family. How would he treat a total stranger?"

"Point." Melinda saved the file and continued working. "I don't know—I was thinking that Arthur was the hallway ghost and that it couldn't be Frederick because Frederick was ice-cold and the ghost is such a screamer, but now I'm starting to wonder. Frederick being the ghost would explain why Florence never left—Daddy wouldn't let her. The sheer malevolence of the spirit sounds more like a Frederick than an Arthur. And now he's hanging around Kevin's B-and-B."

"Doesn't sound like a good place to spend a quiet weekend with the wife." Andrea righted a giraffe. "What do you think he wants?"

Melinda blew out a sigh. "No idea. That's the problem. I hope he doesn't want Florence to forgive him. Hard to arrange, since she's dead."

"Is her ghost around?"

"I haven't seen her."

"That wasn't a denial." Andrea moved on to a rumpled display of rag dolls. "So what's the plan?"

"Tonight I have a check to give Kevin Ray," Melinda said. "And I'll see if I can eke a few more secrets out of the hallway ghost. Whoever it is."

Melinda stood at the entrance to the forbidden hallway, flashlight in hand. Smells of dust and old carpet clogged her nose. Kevin Ray stood beside her, his red hair faded to a dull brown in the bad light. The darkness seemed to stare coldly at Melinda, ordering her back.

"I've been trying all morning to get the electricity in this hallway to work," Kevin said next to her in a hushed voice. "Nothing."

"Stay close," Melinda said. "You're a direct descendant of the man who built this house and maybe of the spirit in this hallway, so it's possible you can get a reaction that I can't."

"This still feels weird," Kevin told her. "It seems so . . . childish. Grown-ups afraid of the dark."

"Being afraid of the dark goes way back," Melinda said. "Back to caveman days, when the dark hid things that might leap out and eat you. It's not stupid—it's survival."

"So why are we going in there?"

"Because we're stupid." Melinda took a tentative step forward. "Hello? Mr. Ray, is that you? I have your great-something-grandson or nephew Kevin with me. I can help you talk to him, if that's what you want. Are you there?"

Kevin and Melinda moved cautiously down the hallway. Melinda kept the flashlight pointed down, allowing them to see without, she hoped, keeping the spirit at bay. Not that the flashlight had frightened it away earlier, but she felt better for trying.

"Say something," Melinda urged.

"Uh, Grandpa Frederick? Uncle Arthur?" Kevin hazarded. "I'm Kevin. Grandma Florence left me the house. Is there a problem I can help with?"

The hall remained empty and dark. Not a shadow moved. Melinda waited a moment, then stepped forward again. "You're frightening a lot of people," she said. "We just want to help. We just want to find out what's wrong and set it right."

No response. Melinda and Kevin edged farther down the forbidden hallway, though Melinda took care to stay out of range of the closet door. Kevin leaned against a section of blank plaster and chewed his lower lip.

"Look, this is just getting ridic—"

The walls and floor shivered. Dust rose up from the faded blue runner. Down the hallway, the closet door slammed open and shut, open and shut, a shutter caught in a windstorm. The temperature plunged, and Melinda saw her breath hanging in the air like a death mask. A low rumbling vibrated beneath her feet. Melinda tried to push down the rising fear, but it reached up past her stomach and clutched at her heart with freezing fingers.

"Is this . . . is this normal?" Kevin whispered. His face was pale, and the flashlight threw ghoulish shadows across his face. "Do you see this a lot?"

A ragged white figure burst through the wall and roared in Kevin's face. Both he and Melinda screamed. The figure swiped a cold hand through Kevin's body, and he grabbed at his chest. His scream faded to a gasp.

"The grave is empty, you fool!" the spirit screeched. *"Run! RUN!"*

Melinda grabbed Kevin's arm and ran. He lurched behind her, gasping and wheezing down a corridor that grew longer with every step. Melinda felt the spirit's cold breath on her neck. She had dropped the flashlight and it had gone out. The shadows were chasing her with the spirit. Run, run, run, that was all there was. Why was the hallway so long? Kevin was a dead weight pulling her back, but she couldn't let go.

"RUN!"

She ran, breathing and panting and dragging Kevin with her. Every step was agony. Every moment was terror.

And then she was at the stairs. Buttery autumn sunlight from the landing window washed over her and Kevin, melting the shadows that clung to them. Melinda glanced down the dark hallway. Empty. Kevin clung to the bannister, wheezing like a man three times his age. Alarmed, Melinda bent over him and saw his teeth were chattering. His skin was icy.

"Are you all right?" she asked. "Should I call an ambulance?"

"I'm cold," he said. "Freezing."

"Can you breathe all right?"

"I . . . think so." He straightened and his breathing eased. "What the hell was that?"

"Let's get you downstairs and into the kitchen," she said. "You need a hot drink and a blanket."

A few minutes later, Kevin was sitting at the kitchen table, wrapped in a blanket with a cup of hot tea in front of him. Also on the table was the check Melinda had brought over earlier. Kevin sipped cautiously, and a little color had returned to his face.

"Did you hear it?" Melinda said. "What happened to you?"

"I felt . . . cold. Arctic cold. Graveyard cold." Kevin shuddered and drank again. "It ripped through me. And I heard a voice telling me the grave was empty. Jesus. I couldn't move, I couldn't breathe, I couldn't think. What kind of monster is it?"

"It's just a spirit," Melinda said. "Scared or angry or confused, but just a spirit."

"Dammit, that's not it!" Kevin slammed a fist on the tabletop. His cup jumped and clattered on the wood. "It's a monster. It's eating at my house. It's attacked both me and my wife. Apparently it's been haunting my family for generations. I need to get it out of my house!"

"You're . . . upset," Melinda said, remembering just in time how touchy he'd been about the word *scared*. "I can understand that. But these things take time to deal with."

"I don't *have* time," Kevin said. "I have to get this house in shape, and that . . . *thing* is getting in the way. I can't do wiring work in that part of the house, I can't clean or sand the floors, and I can't get to one of the bedrooms without going all the way upstairs and down again. Not to mention the fact that I don't dare bring my little girl over here with that thing pissed off."

"I'm sorry," Melinda said. "I'll keep trying. Is there anything else about your family history that might help? Anything you haven't mentioned or maybe haven't remembered until now?"

"No."

"Any idea what the spirit meant when it said the grave is empty?"

"No."

"Are you sure? Think carefully—this could help. Is there a family legend about an empty grave? What about your grandma Florence? Is her grave empty?"

"I saw them close her coffin with her body in it and lower the whole thing into the ground. And there's no family legend about an empty grave." Kevin rose, picked up the check Melinda had brought, and stared at it for a long moment. Then he folded it once and tucked it into his pocket. "Look, I need to move around, do something *real*. Let me know if you need any help with the antiques."

"Of course. And I'll try again with the spirit in a while. Maybe it'll talk without you there."

"Not now," Kevin said quickly. "I'm going to

work on the third floor, and I don't want it getting mad again and deciding to expand its territory."

Melinda spread her hands. First he said he couldn't wait to get rid of the ghost, then he put her off. Well, it was his house, and the ghost certainly didn't seem very communicative today—or ever. "Sure, all right. I'll probably be here another hour before heading home, and I'll come back late tomorrow afternoon. I'm waiting to hear back on two pieces of furniture, incidentally, and I think the price will be really good."

"Great. Keep me updated."

Melinda watched him head for the door. Something had shifted, but she couldn't put her finger on what. That Kevin was unhappy about the spirit was obvious, had been from the beginning, but something else had changed. She wanted to run after him and ask, but knew that would be pointless. Not only did she not know him well enough, she doubted Kevin would be the type to confide. Best instead to concentrate on the house's antiques.

The spirit remained quiet for the rest of the evening, and Melinda returned home, hungry and wiped out. Jim was on second shift, so she scrounged up salad fixings and found some leftover chicken in the refrigerator. Perfect! A little microwaved heat for the chicken, and she was good to go—warm chicken on cool lettuce with crisp cu-

cumbers. Add a splash of some spicy dressing she couldn't identify because the label had fallen off, and it made a perfect supper. It was probably even healthy. She felt proud of herself as she rinsed the dishes and put them in the washer. It was the sort of meal Jim would have assembled. He was the acknowledged head chef in the house, and when he wasn't around, Melinda's taste in dinners leaned toward simple and healthy.

She was just popping a DVD out of its case when the vision crashed over her.

An iron hand shoved Melinda backward into a dark closet with a hard wooden floor. Frightened, she looked up into Father's icy, angry face. She was gasping for breath, and she felt the fabric of her shirt collar still bunched around her neck where Father had tightened it, choking her. Her body ached from a recent beating. And she wasn't Melinda. She was a young boy.

"You'll stay in there until you learn to act like a man," Father hissed. The door slammed, plunging the closet into heavy darkness. Only a thin line of light showed near the bottom of the door. The key clicked in the lock, and footsteps thumped away. Arthur knelt in the corner and tried not to cry, but fear and sadness filled him up and spilled down his face. The darkness and the coffin-size space were impossible to bear. The floorboards pressed against his knees, and even though he was ten years old, his thumb stole into his mouth. He let it. No one would see in here. He didn't cry out. There was no point. Despair weighed him down, and he knelt in the darkness, new bruises aching, trying not to care, to let the time pass without noticing. But he had no idea how long he'd been in the dreadful darkness, nor how long he would be. His legs cramped and he shifted position, but his thumb stayed in his mouth. His stomach rumbled. At least he didn't have to go to the bathroom. Yet.

"Arthur?" whispered a voice at the keyhole.

Arthur straightened and a tiny bit of hope flared. He pulled his thumb from his mouth. "Flo?"

"Shh! Listen, Father's on a real tear. What did you do?"

"Father was going to evict Mrs. Greenlowe. I snuck over there and gave her my Christmas and birthday money, but Father found out. He took it away from her and told me I needed to act like a man instead of a whiny woman." Arthur's voice cracked. "I'm scared, Flo. I'm scared in here."

"I know. I hate him, Arthur. One day someone will lock *him* in forever and ever and see how he likes it."

"It's dark," he said. "I'm scared of the dark. *He* makes me scared of it."

"Here." There was a scratching sound and the crack of light under the door dimmed for a moment as a small box of matches skittered under the door. "When it gets really bad, use one of these. Just be careful."

Arthur gratefully snatched up the box. "I will. Thank you, Flo."

But Florence was already gone. Melinda scratched one of the matches across the floor and the darkness vanished in a flare of bright light. When it cleared, the closet was gone. This time she was a young woman, thirteen or fourteen, lying in a bed, a strange bed, not her own. The quilt was old and worn, the mattress saggy, the pillow lumpy. The sickroom, used when someone fell ill, was dark and narrow, with only a single small window to let in the light and not even a rag rug on the bare floor. The rickety table by her bed held a glass of water and a plate with a few toast crumbs on it. Melinda—no, Florence—felt sweaty and feverish. Her hands and arms were stretched out before her, and they were covered in bloody-looking blisters. Fear washed over her. Was she going to die? Father stood in the doorway, his hand on the knob.

"Don't!" Florence said. "Please don't leave me alone!"

"You can't be allowed to contaminate anyone else," Father said in his ever-calm voice. "You know that."

And before she could say another word, he left the room and locked the door. The key clicked with the sound of a skeleton's finger dragging over stone.

Melinda found herself standing in her own living room, the DVD in one hand, the case in the other. She took a moment and concentrated on the sensations around her—the smooth plastic of the case in her hand, the rainbow light skimming around the DVD, the soft carpet beneath her feet, the air filling her lungs, the faint scent of reheated chicken in the air. She was Melinda Gordon, not Arthur or Florence Ray. She was in her own house, in her own living room, holding her own DVD.

She set the DVD down and sank to the sofa to think. The vision was puzzling. It was a complement to the one she had received in the Ray house kitchen earlier, but it created more questions. Melinda received visions from three sources—ghosts, objects, and places. Melinda had assumed her first vision had come from the kitchen or the kitchen table, since the vision started with Florence hiding there. But now Melinda was nowhere near the Ray house, and she didn't have any objects from the Ray house with her. That left a spirit as the source of the vision. But the visions had come from two different points of view—Uncle Arthur's and Grandma Florence's. Were *both* their spirits still hanging around? It meant that Arthur had to be the hallway ghost, and that Frederick wasn't hanging around. Melinda hadn't seen Florence anywhere, but that didn't mean anything. She might be hiding or unable to manifest fully or tied to a particular spot, one Melinda hadn't visited.

Unfortunately, it meant that Melinda now had two spirits to cross over when before she'd only had one.

With a sigh, Melinda slotted the DVD into the player, plunked back down on the couch, and completely failed to lose herself in the movie.

Late the next afternoon, Melinda left Andrea in charge of the store again and drove out to the Ray house. Most of the first floor was finished. The furniture was cataloged, and most of the small antiques were at the store. Tonight, Melinda intended to take away the rest of the small antiques in her SUV and get a start on the second floor—or whatever parts of it Arthur's ghost would let her reach. And perhaps Kevin would let her have another run at the spirit while she was at it.

Stranded ghosts bugged Melinda. They were like hangnails that needed trimming or an itch that begged to be scratched, only they were a hundred times worse. Arthur's spirit bothered Melinda on many levels because she still knew so little about him. Even Dina Mazurek had yielded her secrets after some patient research, but this ghost was going out of its way to be angry and destructive, far more so than most. It was almost as if he didn't want anyone to help.

Melinda's hands jerked on the steering wheel and she nearly lost control of the SUV. Was that it? Was Arthur deliberately trying to push everyone away because he didn't want help? Melinda continued driving more safely and turned the idea over in her mind. It made sense. She had encountered such spirits before, though only rarely. Most spirits wanted to resolve their problems and move on, but a few wanted to hang around and make life miserable for a particular person, often out of a desire for revenge. But Melinda hadn't felt a thirst for revenge from Arthur, or a need to punish, or even the tiniest bit of hatred. The overwhelming emotion she felt from him every time was fear. If Arthur was hanging around out of fear, what was scaring him so badly? And why hang around if he was afraid? It seemed to Melinda that it would be easier to cross into the Light and leave the fear behind like an old coat that didn't fit or shoes that pinched.

Maybe Melinda was going about this the wrong way. Maybe she needed to figure out what was frightening Arthur's spirit and deal with that. Once the source of fear was gone, Arthur could cross over and Kevin would be left in peace.

Melinda pulled up to the tall, spiky Ray house,

then stomped on the brakes with a sharp gasp. Her tires screeched in protest, and her momentum flung her against the seat belt. Melinda stared, open-mouthed. Wendy King's red Saturn Sky sat parked in the Ray house driveway.

9

No!" Melinda climbed out of her SUV and ran up the overgrown walk. Tension tightened her stomach and constricted her chest. "No no no no no no no."

She barreled into the house and pounded up the stairs. Already the smell of incense had permeated the air. At the top of the stairs to the second floor she found Kevin with Sally standing next to him. They were looking down the forbidden hallway, but turned toward Melinda when they heard her on the steps. Sally gave Kevin a hard look and Kevin looked uncomfortable but determined. Melinda crested the stairs.

"She's here, isn't she?" Melinda panted. "You can't do this, Kevin."

"Melinda—"

"Leave them alone." Wendy's low voice cut

through the dim hallway with the ease of a sharp knife. "I'm here to help them."

She stepped forward out of the shadows of the forbidden hallway, her gray suit blending with the shadows like cobwebs. Her eyes, hard as slate, met Melinda's brown ones. Behind Wendy stood the blurred, bearded figure of her father. The darkness crept into him, invading his borders. Devouring him. Melinda hardened her jaw.

"Mr. Ray called me, but my spirit guide was already leading me here," Wendy said. "The spirit is disrupting his life. As usual, you haven't been able to help him or his family, so I'm here."

Melinda rounded on Kevin. "Kevin, you can't let her work here. She hurts spirits. She terrorizes and tortures them. It's monstrous and painful for everyone."

"It's been monstrous and painful for me and for Sally," Kevin said. "I want that thing out of here, and if she can do it, I'm happy to have her."

Frustration twisted Melinda's insides and her fingernails dug into the palms of her hands. Behind her, Melinda heard the click of a barbecue lighter. Wendy was igniting candles on a folding table she had set up near the front of the hallway, setting shadows to dancing. An incense burner was already going, and now Melinda could see the smoke as well as smell it. The skull was there, along with the book, the silver knife, and the brass bowl on its red silk cushion.

"Kev," Sally said, "I'm still not so sure. Maybe we should talk about this some more with Melinda. And the money Wendy's charging—it's not cheap."

"I got that check," he said. "It's covered."

And Melinda remembered the check she had written Kevin for the antiques she had sold for him at Same As It Never Was. Her stomach churned with nausea. Kevin had gotten the money to pay Wendy, however indirectly, from her.

"Besides," Kevin continued, "that thing attacked you and me. It's evil. I want it out of my house."

"There's more to it than that," Melinda told him. "There always is. Listen to me—we just need some more time."

"I don't have more time." Kevin folded heavily muscled forearms across his chest. "I'm done waiting, I'm done tiptoeing around, and I'm done living as a hostage to that damn ghost."

Wendy struck the brass bowl with the wooden striker. A clear, bell-like tone rang through the hallway, and the dancing shadows seemed to draw away from it. Blue and green lights crawled out of the bowl and skittered down the legs of the table like hungry goblins. Wendy looked down at the open book and began a low, tuneless chant.

Melinda was seized with a desire to sweep the para-phenalia from the table and disrupt what Wendy was doing, but she knew it wouldn't help. Not only would that just get her barred from Kevin's house, it would delay Wendy for only a few minutes while Kevin threw Melinda out and she started over. The air grew thick and heavy as Wendy chanted.

"I don't like this," Sally said. She was hugging herself. "Kevin, tell her to stop."

"I've paid her half in advance," Kevin said. "And I don't *want* her to stop."

A breath of cold air brushed over Melinda's face, and a white figure burst through the wall in the corridor. It rushed up the hallway toward Wendy, its ragged hands reaching for her. A horrible howl tore the air. Despite her dislike for Wendy, Melinda automatically stepped forward to interfere, but before she could do anything more than move, the spirit of Wendy's father appeared before the ghost. He slammed a hand out like a cop order-ing a car to stop. Blue and green sparks flew every-where, and the white figure crashed to a halt as if it had smacked into a wall. Melinda felt the hallway ghost's pain and flinched. She abandoned Kevin and Sally and ran past the table to confront the ghost. It was clawing ineffectually at the air while Wendy's father stood impassive as a statue between it and his daughter. Wendy struck the bowl again and the hallway ghost screamed. A wave of pain crashed over Melinda and her knees wobbled, but she braced a hand against the wall and kept going.

She reached the ghost. "Arthur," she said softly. "Arthur, listen to me."

And at the sound of Melinda speaking his name, the ghost shifted. It changed into a young man, not yet thirty. He had short blond hair, a pug nose, and a long jaw. He wore a collared work shirt rolled to the elbows, brown corduroy trousers, and work boots. The clothes were burned half off him. Patches of skin were blackened and burned. Cracks showed pink flesh and oozed blood. When he turned toward Melinda, she saw half his face had been horribly charred, the blond hair scorched away. Melinda remembered that Arthur had died when a boiler exploded on a construction site. She struggled to keep her face straight.

"Arthur," she said again, "listen to me. I can't stop Wendy from forcing you to cross over. It's going to be painful. Let me help you. What do you need? Hurry! You have to tell me!"

Wendy struck the bowl a third time. Arthur put his hands to his ruined face and screamed. It felt like a knife was slashing through Melinda's heart and lungs. She braced herself against the wall, struggling to stay upright under the onslaught of Arthur's pain. A silver thread spun itself from Arthur's chest. It looped through the air several times and drifted back into the shadows of the hallway

Arthur had haunted for generations. It seemed to disappear into one of the walls.

"Arthur, tell me!" Melinda gasped. "Let me help you cross over now, before Wendy hurts you more."

"*I have to stay,*" Arthur howled. "*I will stay!*" He lunged for Wendy's father, but Wendy's father snatched a loop of the silver thread. The sick violation Melinda had felt at the Xings' apartment returned, and acid burned at the back of her throat as her gorge rose. Arthur staggered. His burned flesh cracked anew. Wendy continued her toneless chant, completely ignoring Melinda. Sally and Kevin were involved in a whispered conversation near the stairs. They seemed to be arguing.

"Why?" Melinda asked hurriedly. "Why do you have to stay? Tell me, and maybe I can help you. I can change whatever it is that's making you stay."

Wendy's father carried a loop of the silver thread over to the table where Wendy was chanting over her bowl. The other end stretched from the wall that anchored it down the dark hallway. Wendy picked up the silver knife and waved it through the flame of one of the candles three times. It began to glow with a green-blue energy that strengthened each time she waved it.

"I release you," Wendy intoned. Her eyes were blank, just as they had been when she had cut Dina Mazurek's thread. She waved the knife, and it left a poison-green trail in the air. "Go into the Light, shining one. By blaze and bell and bowl, I command you. Leave this place!"

"Tell me!" Melinda pleaded. "Please! I can help you."

In response, Arthur spread his arms and screamed. The entire house shook. The floor vibrated, and dust rose from the runner. Plaster fell from the ceiling. Two candles tipped over on Wendy's table, and she righted them without halting her chant. Doors up and down the hallway crashed open and shut. A terrible force slammed Melinda against the wall, squeezed the air from her lungs. She was aware that Kevin and Sally had been flung to the floor but Wendy stood in an island of calm at her candle-lit table. The wall buckled under the force of Arthur's scream. Cracks appeared in the plaster above the wainscoting and spiderwebbed down the hall. The house creaked and shivered. Wendy's father calmly held out a loop of thread before his daughter with one hand. Wendy raised her knife. Her father guided her hand a little to the left.

"I cut your ties to this place," Wendy King chanted. "Go into the Light. You have no more business here."

"*That light!*" Arthur screamed. "*It burns. Oh God—it burns!*"

"No!" Melinda tried to shout, but it came out as a weakened gasp. "No!"

Wendy brought the knife down. It touched the thread. In a flash of light, it parted and vanished. Pain tore Melinda in half. Razors and hot knives sliced her insides. Acid burned her, fire roasted her and split her skin. She couldn't even scream. Arthur did it for her. He clapped both charred hands over his ruined ears and screamed and screamed and screamed. The walls trembled again—

—and then he was gone. The pain vanished as if it had never been, leaving Melinda weak and drained. She dragged herself to her feet and leaned against the cracked plaster wall, trying to pull herself together.

And then Sally was there, helping her up. "Are you all right?" she said.

"I will be," Melinda told her. Only then did she realize tears were running down her cheeks. "But it'll take a long while."

"Your visitor is gone," Wendy said. She was already packing her things into a duffel bag, leaving the candles behind as she had done before. The spirit of her father was nowhere to be seen. Kevin stood at the front of the hallway, looking uncertain.

"How do you know?" he said.

Wendy gestured at the hall. "Check for yourself. Turn on the lights. Walk down the hall."

Hesitantly, Kevin reached for the old-fashioned light switch and pressed it. With a click, normal light flooded the hallway. Melinda and Sally both turned to look. The faded blue runner merely looked old and tired on the scarred wooden floor. The doors hung open to reveal perfectly ordinary rooms beyond. Except for the heavily cracked plaster, there wasn't a sign of anything out of the ordinary.

"Wow," Kevin said. "I don't think I've ever seen it with the lights on like this."

Wendy zipped her bag shut. "You may keep the candles. I can only use them once. And there's the matter of the other half."

Kevin blinked at her. "Other half?"

"Of my fee."

"Oh! Right!" He pulled some folded bills out of his pocket and handed them to her. Wendy pocketed them with a thank you, gave Melinda a small, stony smile, and trotted down the stairs with neat, tiny steps. The front door opened and shut.

Rage swept over Melinda. Her hands shook with it and small red spots hovered at the edges of her vision. Kevin, apparently seeing the expression on her face, put up his hands.

"Look, I had to," he said. "I was scared that thing would attack us again. Then I saw this business card in the wastebasket." He pulled the familiar scrap of pasteboard from his shirt pocket and held it up. "I didn't remember throwing it away, so I pulled it out to take a look and decided to call her."

Melinda froze. A sick feeling oozed through her stomach. She had led Kevin to Wendy and had provided him with the means to pay her, all at once. Suddenly the dingy hallway felt crowded and stifling.

"I have to get out of here," she said, and fled the hallway. Without knowing why, she ran through the kitchen and out the back door into the backyard. The long grass swept at her bare calves beneath her skirt. The bright autumn breeze was a welcome change from the murky house, and she greedily sucked in the cool air, then forced it out, trying to expel mingled fear and pain and anger with every exhalation. Her feet slammed into the earth as if punishing it. Everything was going wrong. Every person she tried to help was getting hurt instead. Arthur's burned spirit had no chance to heal, no chance to find closure with his family. And it was at least partly Melinda's fault.

After a while, she realized she was treading an overgrown path that led away from the house. The backyard sloped gently away from the main house, and Melinda passed outbuildings in various stages of disrepair and disuse. Overgrown bushes and tall trees alternately blocked the sun or let it come down. The leaves were turning now, showing the beginnings of scarlets and golds. The path was marked with flat paving stones that were overgrown with grass and moss. The farther Melinda walked, the closer in the trees and bushes grew, until she found herself walking through woods instead of overgrown garden. The grass showed signs of trampling by a large group of people, and she wondered who else had been back here. A group of teenagers using the area as a makeout point?

Melinda rounded a curve in the wooded path and came upon a decent-size clearing bordered by sad-looking willow trees and heavy brush. Green and gold light filtered down through the leaves, giving the place an otherworldly feel. The ground was peppered with gravestones. Most were mossy and crumbling. The name *Ray* was prominent on all of them. Melinda halted, surprised, then annoyed that she was surprised. It wasn't at all unusual for a wealthy old family to have a family plot tucked away on their own property. In fact, it seemed likely she would find . . . yes. A fairly fresh grave. Grass was growing on it, but thinly, and the dirt was still mounded. The marker was also brand-new. Melinda easily read it: FLORENCE RAY, along with her birth and death dates. The much older grave next to hers was for ARTHUR RAY, BELOVED BROTHER AND SON. One grave over from that, Melinda found graves for REGINA RAY, DEAR WIFE, who had died before her thirtieth birthday, and Frederick Ray, who had nothing on his stone except the dates. His grave had collapsed, leaving a coffin-size indentation about six inches deep. A chill came over Melinda as she stared down at it.

"'Beloved Brother and Son.' Hm! Father insisted on putting that on the gravestone, even though he didn't care about Arthur one way or the other."

Melinda turned. An old woman, possibly the oldest Melinda had ever seen, was standing behind her. Her gray hair was pulled back in a long ponytail, and she wore a faded blue housedress with tennis shoes. She was as wrinkled as an old plum, and she leaned on a cane of carved ivory. Gnarled knuckles bumbled about under spotted papery skin as she shifted her weight and moved the cane to compensate. Melinda blinked. Contrary to popular thought, it was unusual to find ghosts in cemeteries. Spirits fed on energy from the living, and there wasn't much of that in the average graveyard.

"Florence Ray?" Melinda asked.

"Call me Flo," the old woman said in a crackly old voice. *"I've been waiting for you, sweetie. I have a few things to tell you."*

Melinda remembered her visions. At least one had come from Flo's point of view, and it was clear now that it had come from her, and not from the house. "How did you know I was coming?"

"I didn't know it would be you specifically, sweetie. Not at first. But I knew the right person would come, and after a while I felt you out there. So I waited. Out here. Away from that house. I couldn't get away

from it in life, so I'm waiting out here now that I'm dead." She stumped over to Regina Ray's grave and looked down at it. *"It's hard to stay, though. I can see a shining light at the edge of this graveyard. It's growing brighter by the moment, and my mother is waiting for me in it. I never knew her. I want to talk to her very badly."*

"Then go!" Melinda urged. "Your time here is done. You can move on."

"Hm!" Flo shook her head. *"Not yet, sweetie. You need to know some things."* She pointed with her cane to Frederick's sunken grave. *"I think Arthur tried to tell you that it's empty. And it is. Father was a horrible man, you know. He caused my brother and me nothing but pain."*

"I'm sorry," Melinda said.

"Thank you," Flo replied. *"He punished us in the most horrible ways for the smallest things. Now I can see that he was really trying to punish himself. That explains his behavior, of course, but it doesn't excuse it."*

Melinda said nothing. There were times when she felt she should agree or nod her head, but she had learned not to. People—and spirits—often got angry when an outsider criticized a relative, no matter how deserving or how much criticism the speaker heaped on, and Melinda had learned the best way to handle it was to keep her mouth shut and look attentive.

Flo stared off into the distance for a long moment. *"That light. My mother."* She shook her head. *"Hm! Not yet, woman, not yet. Now listen, sweetie—I finally found a way to stop my father from hurting us. Or so I thought. When I was young, I came down with cowpox. It's very similar to smallpox, and at first everyone thought that's what I had, including Father. He locked me in the sick room so no one else would catch it. I was scared I would die alone, and I begged him not to leave me, but he locked me in anyway. Later I got well, but being locked in that room, alone, thinking I was going to die . . . just as I had been locked in basements and closets and eventually the house itself . . . that was the worst.*

"I wanted Father to love me. I wanted it my entire life. I thought if I could be a good enough daughter, he would. Hm! But after he left me alone to die, I knew he would never love me. In that moment, I knew he hated me. He blamed me for my mother's death, you know. He was a monster who had people maimed or killed so he could buy their land cheaply. Land was all that really mattered to him. Land, and my mother."

Her voice was as dry as old leaves, bereft of emotion. Her ancient eyes remained fixed on a point in the distance. The Light was growing brighter for her, and Melinda could feel Flo's desire to leave the pain and bad memories behind.

"Cowpox makes you immune to smallpox. I don't know if you knew that, sweetie. A few months after Arthur started work, a little girl in town came down with real smallpox. When I heard about it, I volunteered to nurse her. I couldn't catch it, you see, so I was safe. The girl survived it, though her face was scarred with pits and pockmarks. I felt sorry for her. Hm! There was a glass in her bedroom, one she drank from several times. I took it home, filled it with water, and put it by Father's bed in place of his usual night glass. In the morning, the water was gone, and I knew it was just a matter of time."

"Your father came down with smallpox and died," Melinda said.

"Yes. But Arthur and I weren't free. Father knew what I had done, and he knew Arthur was in it with me. He haunted us. He wanted revenge. I heard him whispering at night, and I felt him drawing strength from me. It was the worst feeling—the darkness had finally come for me. I slept with lights on all the time, but it didn't help. And then I got the news of the boiler accident and Arthur's death. I knew Father's spirit was responsible. He had become strong enough to affect the world of the living."

Her gaze grew more distant. *"But after Arthur died, everything changed. Arthur was still with me. I couldn't bring myself to leave the house. Hm! I was still locked in with Arthur."* Flo didn't look at Melinda. Her gaze was fixed on the distance. Her posture straightened, and she dropped the cane. It vanished. Some of her wrinkles faded, and new streaks of black competed with the spidery gray in her long ponytail. *"But the grave is empty. That's what I needed to tell you."* Her expression changed. A bright smile burst across her face and Melinda caught a ray of happiness like sunlight breaking through a dark window. *"Arthur! I see Arthur! He isn't burned! He's grinning like he did when we were young. And my mother is with him. I want to go so badly."*

"Then go," Melinda said. "You've earned it."

Florence gave her a small smile. *"Hm! I think there's one more thing I probably need to do, and then I will. But don't worry about me, sweetie. You have bigger problems than a little old lady in tennis shoes."*

She strode across the graveyard with strong, certain steps and vanished without a backward look. Melinda looked at the empty graveyard, the grass still a bit trampled from Grandma Florence's burial service, and at the sunken grave beneath Frederick Ray's tombstone. She felt a little better. Arthur's crossing had been harsh and horrible, but he was happy now, reunited with his mother, grinning a wash of brilliant light to welcome his sister. It also occurred to her that this was confirmation that Dina and Mr. Xing had definitely crossed over. Doubt she hadn't known she was carrying fell away like lead feathers.

Melinda scuffed the edge of Frederick's grave with her shoe. A bit of moss broke off and fell into the indentation, throwing up a damp forest smell. Arthur had also warned her that the grave was empty. What did it mean? Where was his body? And did it matter? It was over, everything was resolved. Arthur, the hallway ghost, had crossed over, and Grandma Florence would soon follow. There wasn't anything left to deal with except the rest of the antiques in the Ray house.

Melinda made a small grimace. The idea of continuing to work with Kevin Ray no longer appealed to her, no matter how wonderful the antiques. Maybe she should back out of the agreement. There were other antique dealers in the area. She could make a couple of recommendations to soften the blow and go back to the shop.

With these thoughts on her mind, she made her way back along the path and into the house. Kevin immediately accosted her in the kitchen, his face flushed with excitement.

"There you are! You have to see this, Melinda," he said. "You won't believe it."

Without waiting for a reply, he dashed out of the kitchen and up the main stairs. Puzzled, Melinda followed. The second-floor hallway was brightly lit now—Kevin had replaced the low-watt bulbs with more powerful ones—and everything was covered in a layer of plaster dust. Cracks ran across the walls, making them look like the shell of a hard-boiled egg that had been dropped on the floor. The closet door that had smacked Melinda in the face hung open, revealing a tiny, sad-looking space behind. On the floor were scratch marks like those left behind by old-fashioned matches. Melinda thought about the little boy forced to sit inside it in the dark for hours, and her heart twisted in her chest. Kevin strode past it in blissful ignorance. Sally was standing a little way down the hall, examining a blank section of wall. Two more figures waited beside her, one tiny and female, the other tall and familiar.

"Jim?" Melinda said, trotting forward to get a kiss. His presence was puzzling, but it set her more at ease and relaxed her more than she would have expected. "What are you doing here?"

"Kevin called me," Jim replied. He gave Melinda a small smile. "Told me he'd found something at the house that he'd need help with, and he said you were here, so I came over."

"He brought more tools," said the girl Melinda didn't know. She looked to be eight or nine years old, with red-brown hair and Kevin's blue eyes. She wore jeans and a T-shirt and had a set of earbuds tucked into her ears. A white cord ran from them down to her pocket.

"Our daughter, April," Sally said. "Her grandmother dropped her off. Now that Wendy . . . well, it's okay for her to be here now."

"The hallway isn't scary anymore," April said. "And it doesn't short out my player."

Jim pointed to a small pile of tools on the floor nearby—hammers, sledgehammers, and crowbars. "Do we want to get started?"

"I'm ready," Kevin said.

"What is this about?" Melinda asked.

Kevin gestured at the wall. "Look at the cracks in the wall there."

Melinda did. It took her a moment, but then she saw what they were talking about. The cracks formed a pattern—the outline of a doorway above the wainscoting. She ran her hands over the outline. A faint draft of air drifted across her fingertips.

"We measured the bedrooms on either side of it," Sally said. "They aren't long enough to account for the length of the hallway. There's an extra space of about seven feet here. We also looked outside, and there's an extra window in the middle of the second floor. The house is so big that no one noticed the discrepancy."

"Or they never said anything," Melinda muttered, still examining the cracks.

"It's a secret room," April said. Her eyes were alight with excitement. "Maybe there's a treasure in there or a mummy or—"

"Or more likely it's just a walled-over storage closet," Kevin said.

Then Kevin cleared his throat. "Look, I'm sorry if I upset you by calling Wendy. I didn't know you two were rivals."

"Rivals?" Melinda said. "That's not how I would put it." Her earlier anger started to rise like a bloody moon. She should tell him about her conversation with Grandma Florence, but she knew if she said anything, it would come out with a snarl, so she pushed back the words. "Look, I'd just rather not be where she is. Let's leave it at that."

"Wendy King was here?" Jim said.

"I'll tell you about it later," Melinda said. "I have to admit that I'm curious about this room."

Kevin hefted a sledgehammer. "Then stand back." He swung and hit the wall with a loud *crack*. Plaster puffed and lathe shattered. Kevin pulled the hammer out of the hole he had made and peered inside. "Yep. Looks like there's a door here. Give me that crowbar, Jim. We have to pull the wainscoting off."

"Carefully," Jim said. "That's walnut. You don't want to ruin it. You got pliers? We can pull out the nails."

"How long is this going to take?" Sally asked.

"Shouldn't be more than a couple hours," Kevin said.

"Hmmmm," Melinda said. "Fun as this may be, I think I feel a tea attack coming on."

"And I'm getting plaster in my hair," April said.

"Let's go upstairs," Sally said. "Some of the rooms are finished enough to use. We stay there sometimes. Come see what your husband has helped with."

Melinda hadn't really explored the third floor except as a way to get around the second-floor hallway, so she was happy to follow Sally and April upstairs after extracting a promise from Kevin and Jim that they wouldn't open the door without calling the women down first.

"You're the antique lady," April said as they went up the creaky wooden stairs.

"I sure am."

"Is this an antique?" April pulled her MP3 player from her pocket and held it up. "It only has one gig of memory and no video. Maybe it's worth something."

Melinda took the MP3 player and examined it seriously. "I don't think so," she said at last. "But one day it will be. Hold on to it, and when you're a grandma, you can sell it for lots of money."

"Yuck! I don't even want to be a mom!"

"April, don't bother Ms. Gordon," Sally admonished.

"It's all right. I'm happy to get another generation hooked on antiques."

"Easy enough around this house. Here we are."

The third floor consisted of a long hallway with several doors facing it. At the far end, another staircase went back down to the second floor. The floor had been refinished, and the dark wood gleamed. No wainscoting up here, and the walls sported a fresh coat of warm yellow paint. Halfway down the hall, a reading nook opened up, complete with bay window and window seat. The seat was just a bare bench, and footsteps echoed against bare wood and painted plaster.

"We're going to put cushions on the window seat, of course," Sally said, "and throw rugs on the floor. We discussed wallpaper, going for an authentic 1800s look, but realized upkeep would be harder and went with paint instead."

"It looks wonderful," Melinda said. "Very homey."

"Let me show you my room!" April said, grabbing Melinda's hand and towing her toward one of the doors.

The room inside was cozy and done up as a nineteenth-century bedroom. A four-poster bed with a canopy and yellow coverlet sat against one wall. Near the door was a mirror table with a ceramic bowl and pitcher. Sunlight poured in through the windows, which looked out over the overgrown backyard. A few toys were scattered around the room, and an open laptop sat on the bed.

"We stay here sometimes," April said, flopping onto her bed. "It's kind of creepy at night, but during the day it's fun."

"We have a sitting room up here, too, with an electric kettle and tea things," Sally said. "Want something to eat? The cookies involve chocolate."

"Perfect!" Melinda said.

A few minutes later, they were having tea and cookies in a truly old-fashioned parlor. Oriental rugs on the hardwood floor, actual horsehair furniture, and a working fireplace. Melinda felt as if she should be wearing a brooch and bustle. Two of the seats were occupied by large puppets, one boy and one girl. The boy wore a sailor suit. The girl was dressed exactly like April. It even had her hairstyle and two earbuds trailing down to her pocket.

"Is this meant to be you?" Melinda asked. "It's very cute."

"That's April T-o-o," April said. "Mom does custom orders for people. That's one of her demos."

"We're planning to hold regular teas here," Sally was saying, filling Melinda's cup from a china pot. "With parlor games and such. And puppet shows."

"Boring!" April said. She was lying on her stomach in front of her laptop, typing idly with one hand.

"If it doesn't have a modem," Sally said, "it doesn't exist for April. We'll install Wi-Fi, just for guests like her."

"The old and the new can mesh perfectly well," Melinda said with a smile. "The only reason our forefathers and foremothers didn't use computers and other technology was that they weren't available. My grandmother loved to cook, but you can bet she would have been first in line to buy a food processor and bread machine if they'd been around when she was young." She sipped minty tea and glanced at April Too. "How's the puppet business going?"

"Busily. Kevin still thinks he'll be able to get away without hiring a business manager because he thinks I'll be able to handle that, and I keep telling him I already have a full-time job. It's one of his blind spots."

They chatted over more tea. On the floor below, bangs and thumps started up, and one loud crash. April jumped to her feet. "I'm gonna go see!"

"Stay out of their way!" Sally called as she ran for the door.

A few minutes later, April dashed breathlessly back in. "They're ready to open the door," she panted. "Come on!"

The second-floor hallway wasn't as messy as Melinda had expected. Jim and Kevin had cleaned as they worked, stacking walnut wainscoting carefully to one side and sweeping up the plaster and lathe. The newly exposed, dark brown door was scatched and battered from the deconstruction work. It had no knob, allowing it to be plastered over smoothly. Kevin was using the claw end of a hammer to pull out a nail. It came free with a screech.

"It's nailed shut," Jim explained, as if it weren't obvious. "We thought about trying to get through the outside window with a ladder just to see, but that would probably involve breaking the glass, so we decided not to."

"That's the last one," Kevin said, tossing the bent nail into a pile of broken plaster with a clink. "Let's see if we can open this."

He pushed against the door experimentally. It didn't budge. He pushed harder. Nothing. Melinda bent to examine the hole where the knob had been. She tried peering inside and saw nothing but darkness. A faint smell of dust and rotten cloth wafted through the keyhole.

"Let me try this," Jim said. Melinda backed away, and Jim inserted a flat screwdriver into the hole where the knob had been. He turned the screwdriver. Metal screeched and there was a *click*. Jim pushed against the door. Nothing. "It's locked."

"Sally, would you get the key ring?" Kevin asked.

"I know where it is!" April said, and dashed away. She returned moments later with a large ring of old-fashioned iron keys. They jangled like metal teeth as she handed them to Kevin.

"Never thought I'd actually use these," Kevin said. He stuck one in the lock, but it wouldn't turn. He tried a second, a third, and a fourth with the same result. The fifth key, however, turned with a distinctive sound.

The noise of the key brought a sudden dread to Melinda. Her limbs felt heavy and her fingertips felt like little cakes of ice. *The grave is empty.* "Kevin," she said, "I don't think April should be here."

"Why not?" April said.

Melinda turned to Sally. "Maybe April could go upstairs? I think it might be a good idea."

Sally looked ready to object. Then she saw the expression on Melinda's face. "Come on, honey. It's too crowded. We'll look later, okay?"

"Mo-om!"

"*Now,* April. You can show me that unicorn website."

The bribe didn't have much effect on April's mood, and she went upstairs with poor grace. Sally gave Melinda one last glance, and Melinda nodded her thanks as mother and daughter headed up the steps.

"What's going on?" Jim asked.

"It's not going to be good," Melinda said, "and April doesn't need to see."

"What's in there?" Kevin said, one hand braced against the door. "Do you know?"

"I have a suspicion, but I don't know for sure. If it were up to me, I'd wall that door back up and forget it ever existed." Melinda felt odd, like she was half in a trance. Her words were slow and measured. "But that wouldn't help, would it? It's already too late. Far too late. You may as well go in, I think."

Kevin shook his head. "Then let's do this." And he opened the door.

10

THE HINGES SCREECHED and wailed. Kevin shoved the door all the way open with difficulty, poked his head into the darkness beyond, and stepped inside. Jim and Melinda followed.

The room was small and narrow. An iron bedstead took up the back corner near the dusty window. A low dresser along one wall, braided rag rug next to the bed, night table near the rug. On the night table stood an oil lamp, water glass, a pair of metal-framed eyeglasses, and two old-fashioned medicine bottles made of glass. White pills filled one halfway, and gray powder coated the bottom of the other. The bed was lumpy and unmade, the blankets piled into an unwieldy mountain. A tall, skinny wardrobe provided closet space. A pair of carpet slippers sat on the rug near the bed. Dust coated everything and motes of it hung like mummified insects in the dim slant of light that crept in through the window. Smells of mold and old cloth drifted on a slight draft that chilled the room.

The three people looked cautiously about. A small part of Melinda's mind was totaling up the potential worth of the antiques in the room and coming up with a large figure. After a moment, Kevin said, "I don't know what I was expecting, but this wasn't it."

Melinda drifted over to the bed, pulled there by a compulsion she didn't quite understand. The mounded blankets were gray wool, the pillowcase a dusty yellow cotton. With a hand that wasn't quite her own, she reached down and yanked the blanket aside. A dry, brown skull stared up at her. Wild wisps of gray hair clung to the top. Yellow teeth grinned at nothing in the thin light, and a dead spider curled its legs inside one of the empty eye sockets. The sight snapped Melinda free of the half trance the room had put her in. She jumped back with a squawk that brought Jim and Kevin straight over.

"Holy shit!" Kevin said. "What the hell is that?"

Jim pulled the blankets farther back. The skeleton was wearing the ragged remains of red-and-white-striped silk pajamas. The bony hands stuck out of the sleeves like brown sticks, and they rattled as the blanket moved. Jim looked down at the skeleton, then at the heavy door. His face was stony. Unease stole over Melinda, replacing her earlier shock.

"What are you thinking?" she asked.

"I think," Jim said, "that this is a plague room."

Kevin, who had drawn away from the bed, blinked at him. "What's a plague room?"

"They used to have them back when highly communicable diseases like smallpox and tuberculosis were common but not well understood," Jim said. "When someone died of a contagious disease, rather than risk getting sick themselves, the survivors sometimes just . . . shut the door."

"Shut the door?" Kevin echoed. "You mean they just left the body in the room?"

Jim shook his head. "Not usually. The main problem was getting rid of the pathogen. People didn't know how to disinfect back then, but they knew that anyone who moved into a room where someone had died of a disease tended to catch it. In big houses like this one, they would sometimes close the room off permanently, even wall it up so no one would go in by accident. Wait a generation, and no one would know the room had ever been there. But sometimes . . . if the disease was really bad or no one was willing to go in and touch the body . . . sometimes they might wall the room up with the corpse still inside."

The grave is empty.

"Wow." Kevin edged back to the bed and looked down at the skeleton. "So who was—is—this?"

"I think it's Frederick Ray," Melinda said.

"My great-great-grandfather? The tyrant who locked Grandma Florence in the cellar when she was a girl?" Kevin said. "He's buried in the family plot."

"No," Melinda said. "I found the family grave-yard out back, but Frederick's grave is empty."

"How do you know? The whole family went out there for Grandma Florence's burial, but we didn't dig anything up."

"I saw his grave had collapsed, and . . ." Melinda hesitated, then plunged on. "I also talked to your grandma Florence. Her spirit was there. She told me that she infected Frederick with smallpox on purpose because he'd abused her and Arthur for years and because it was Frederick's fault Arthur died. She also told me Frederick's grave was empty."

"You talked to Grandma Florence? Was she okay? Did she do that . . . crossing over thing?"

"She's fine," Melinda said. "She seemed to be contented, but she was waiting to cross over. She said she had one more thing to do, and she wouldn't say what it was."

Kevin glared down at the skeleton with contempt. "Looks like they just left Frederick's body in the room when he died. I can understand why. He may have been family, but he was a total bastard."

"They did more than just leave the body here," Jim said quietly. He was standing by the door, peering behind it. "Look."

He swung the heavy door shut, and the hinges screamed again, as if they were in pain. On the inside of the door were long scratch marks that reminded Melinda of the ones Arthur had left on the closet floor. Slender streaks of brown stained some of them, and as the door tapped the jamb, something flaked off the wood and fluttered to the floor like a dying insect. Melinda crouched down to look. It was an old fingernail. Melinda's stomach roiled with nausea. And then in a flash she was wearing striped silk pajamas. Her hands were covered with scabs and bloody boils, and her body was racked with fever. Chills alternated with waves of heat. She pounded on the heavy door with weakened fists, then clawed at it until her fingernails tore. Her blisters burst and spread scarlet over the wood, but her strength was already giving way. Matching thumps and thuds sounded on the other side of the door. Two hammers at work, driving iron nails deep into the wood.

"No!" Melinda rasped.

"Go to sleep, Father," came Florence's voice from the other side, muffled but recognizable.

"It'll all be over soon," added Arthur.

Melinda staggered over to the window and struggled to open it. It didn't budge. She stared down at two nails freshly driven into the frame. When had that been done? All right—she could break the glass, climb through the sash.

A coughing spasm tore her chest. Every movement was a gut-wrenching convulsion that felt like it would tear her soul free of her body. When it was over, a terrible chill swept over her, and her muscles felt like slush drawn over rotten ice. She barely had strength to kick off her slippers and crawl under the blankets. Florence and Arthur. The mean, ungrateful brats had gotten their revenge at last. Hatred burned through Melinda hotter than any fever. Florence had killed dear Regina, and now, despite all the best efforts to raise her right, she had found a way to kill her own father, too. The little slut thought she would get the house, that she would spread her legs for some man and drop her filthy children in the house Melinda (Frederick?) had built with her (his?) money on her (his!) land. And Arthur, too weak to stand up for himself, had gone along with it. Arthur thought he would get the business, the land, the money that Frederick had earned through hard, honest work. But Florence and Arthur were wrong. Frederick could feel his life slipping away, but he wouldn't leave this house, and once he was free of this weakened body, he would destroy both of them. He should have taken care of Florence years ago, when she was a baby, but he had loved her too much, couldn't bring himself to do what needed to be done, had held out the hope that he could bring her up to be a proper lady who would treat him with proper respect. He should have sent Arthur away to military school, but he had held out the hope that he himself could make a man out of the boy. The boy had proved weak and mewling. A tenant's smallest sob story was enough to break him. He would let go of the land at any pretext, no matter how hard Frederick beat the lessons into him.

His breathing grew weaker. Air rattled emptily in his lungs and his heartbeat grew sluggish. It wouldn't end this way. He wouldn't allow it. He was Frederick Ray, dammit! His own children turning on him like this—didn't they understand that everything Frederick had done, he had done out of love? He had loved Florence too much to kill her, even though she had killed her own mother in the birthing bed. He had loved Arthur so much that he had kept him at home instead of sending him away. And still they betrayed him at every turn.

The hammer blows continued to fall, dull thumps that echoed his slowing heart. A part of him knew that when the last blow fell, his life would end. Now that Frederick had seen the depth of his children's ingratitude, he felt his love change to something else, something heavy and black. A part of him was growing lighter, wanted to drift away like a carefree feather on a warm updraft. But the new emotion weighed him down, held him like an anchor made of lead and granite. For a moment he hung suspended between the two, heavy and light, feather and lead. He could choose. It was up to him.

Another nail drove into the door. Frederick made his choice. He clutched at the anchor and felt its crushing weight pull him down. He was vaguely aware of weakness, and he held on to the weight with all his strength to keep from drifting away. He remembered his hatred for Arthur.

The world shifted, moved, became blurry, like a half-remembered dream. Frederick moved through this hazy new place, barely able to function. Objects wouldn't respond to his touch, and for long periods, he could barely see or hear. Voices babbled in the distance, growing louder and fading away as if in a fog. Eventually he became aware of Arthur's presence. Arthur was at work, on a job site. Building something on Frederick's land. Frederick's hatred grew, and he was able to draw strength from somewhere. He wanted to hurt Arthur, and he lashed out with his hatred, but it did nothing. He tried again and again, but he couldn't see what he was doing most of time. He was locked in—or out. Eventually his hands found a bolt on a boiler. It was a familiar shape, and he knew that Arthur often spent time near the machine. Frederick fastened all his concentration on the tiny metal object. He shifted it, twisted it, stole energy to move it. It fell away and vanished, but Frederick found another one, and then another. Exhausted, he fell back into the strange haze that continually surrounded him to rest.

Some time later, he became aware of certain impressions. A terrible explosion that passed harmlessly through him. A body flung far away. His own feeling of exultation. The sound of weeping. Funeral songs. All of it gave him more strength, more awareness. The haze cleared and the world sharpened. He could see Florence weeping at the fresh mound of dirt beneath a stone that bore Arthur's name. Frederick smiled with righteous glee. So Arthur was dead. The bastard had paid the ultimate price for betraying his father. Frederick drifted back to the bed where his body lay and gloated. Florence was still in the house, and he would see to her next.

"Hello, Father."

Frederick Ray stared in sick amazement. Arthur sat on the end of the sickroom bed. He was wearing the blue work shirt and brown corduroys he had died in. Half his face was a mangled, burned mass of meat, and Frederick smelled singed hair and skin.

"I know you can see me," Arthur said. "And I know what you did to me. I won't let you hurt Flo, Father. You got me, but you won't get her." He backed toward the door, half a smile twisting his ruined face. "We'll lock you in, body *and* soul." He stepped through the door and was gone.

Fury gripped Frederick. In an instant, he was on his feet. He rushed toward the door, full of might and power. He slammed into it with the strength of a bull. Pain crashed through his shoulder and he rebounded onto the floor. Roaring with rage, he slammed against the door again and again and again, but it didn't even quiver. He dashed for the window, then pulled up short. Lying on the bed was a sad lump of blankets. His own face, bloated with decay, stared up at the ceiling. He was dead. Enraged, he flung himself at the bed, but only managed to flip a corner of the blanket over his grotesque features. He drew back a fist to punch the window, but suddenly Arthur was there, hanging just outside the glass, staring in at him with one ruined eye. His stare drained Frederick of his strength, but not his anger. That only grew stronger. He slumped to the floor and didn't move even when he heard Florence directing the servants to plaster over the door.

He would wait. And his anger grew.

Melinda staggered and caught the bedpost for support. She wanted to sit down, but the only available place was the bed, and nothing would have persuaded her to take up a seat there.

"A vision?" Jim said.

Melinda nodded and quickly filled them in. "Florence and Arthur didn't lock the door after Frederick died," she finished.

Sudden understanding crossed Kevin's face. "They did it before," he said.

A cold wind tore through the room. The blankets flew off the bed and bones rattled. Melinda heard harsh laughter rasping like a cough. An evil smell rose on the wind and tugged at Melinda's hair.

"We need to get out of here," Melinda said. "Now!"

No one needed urging. Everyone hurried for the door and Kevin slammed it shut behind them. The tongue caught in the groove, and it stayed shut even without the knob.

"What's going on?" Kevin said. "Wendy got rid of the hallway ghost. It was Arthur, right?"

"She did," Melinda said. The effects of the vision were wearing off, and everything was coming together now. It became more and more clear as she spoke, and she felt tension twist her stomach. "But there's more to it than that. Come on—we have to see if Sally and April are all right."

She hurried toward the stairs. Kevin and Jim followed her, wide-eyed. "Florence purposefully infected her father with smallpox and then she and Arthur locked him up in that room once he was too weak to do anything about it. They locked him in as an adult just like he'd locked them in when they were children. They buried an empty coffin and sealed off the room, partly so no one else would get sick, but mostly to punish Frederick the way he had punished them. But when Frederick finally died, his angry spirit became even angrier and went after Arthur. That's what caused the boiler to explode in the 'accident' that killed Arthur. Frederick was going to go after Florence next, but Arthur stayed behind to protect her. Arthur's ghost kept Frederick's spirit in the plague room and kept everyone else out of it. That's why Arthur wouldn't talk to me and why Arthur wouldn't leave. He couldn't let anyone find out about that room. Florence was the only living person left who knew about it, and she wasn't telling. It's why she almost never left the house and why she didn't sell the place—a new owner might find that room and open it. If the original servants suspected anything, they kept their mouths shut. They probably hated and feared Frederick Ray as much as she did."

They were climbing the stairs to the third floor now. Melinda could still hear faint, raspy laughter from the second floor. Behind her, Jim coughed hard, and Kevin cleared his throat heavily.

"Arthur didn't haunt the hallway because he didn't want to cross over," Melinda said. "He haunted the hallway to protect your family. Despite what his father thought of him, Arthur knew he was the only one strong enough to stop his father, stop Frederick Ray from hurting anyone ever again. But now Arthur's gone, and there's no one to keep Frederick in check."

They reached the third-floor landing, and Melinda realized both Jim and Kevin were wheezing. She turned and stared. A red rash was making its way over Jim's face. He was flushed with fever and his eyes were bright. Kevin was showing the same symptoms. Even as Melinda watched, the individual red spots grew larger and more numerous.

"I don't feel good," Kevin said. "I feel awful."

Jim leaned against the bannister. "So do I. What's wrong with me?" He looked down at his hands. The rash had spread there, too. "What is this?"

"Smallpox." Melinda breathed. "Oh my God. Jim! We have to get you and Kevin to bed."

She took Jim's arm and led him toward one of the bedrooms. Kevin followed, staggering as he went. Melinda wanted to help him, too, but she had only one set of hands. She pushed open the first door she came to and found a guest room with two twin beds in it. The mattresses were bare and the furniture was draped with slipcovers, but it was a place to lie down. She got Jim onto one mattress. Kevin flopped onto the other. Melinda jerked open the closet and found blankets. Both men were shivering uncontrollably. Panic clawed at Melinda's gut and squeezed her heart, but she forced herself to stay calm. Plenty of time for freaking out after the crisis was over. One thing at a time. Get the guys warmed up. Check on April and Sally. Deal with the ghost.

"I can't have smallpox," Jim protested feebly. "I've been vaccinated."

Melinda threw two blankets over him. They smelled like mothballs. Jim curled up, shivering. The rash was getting worse, and his forehead was burning hot to her touch. His fever must be well over a hundred. But it was impossible. Somehow Frederick Ray's ghost had managed to reach into their minds, convincing Jim and the Rays that they were in the grip of smallpox fever. It seemed impossible, but Melinda knew that a spirit as powerful as Frederick Ray actually could make them believe they were dying.

She kissed Jim quickly, then turned to fling a pair of blankets over Kevin, who looked at her with feverish eyes.

"What's going on?" he whispered. "I don't understand."

"It's Frederick," she said. "You stay here and rest. I'll take care of it." She sounded more confident than she felt.

"Why aren't you sick?" Kevin asked. His voice was as thin as burned paper.

"It's because of my talent. Stay here. I'll check on—"

"Sally! April!" Kevin tried to get up. He managed to get to his elbows, then swayed dizzily and fell back onto the bed. The angry red rash on his face was growing worse.

"Stay there," Melinda ordered. "I'll check on them."

"April . . ." Kevin shivered. "Don't let anything happen . . . to April . . ."

Melinda gave Jim one last look—he seemed to have fallen into a restless sleep—and dashed out of the room. She ran up the hall to the sitting room. Sally and April were huddled under afghans, Sally on the sofa, April on the love seat. The puppets, including April Too, lay sprawled on the floor. Both Sally and April were covered with smallpox sores. April seemed to be deeply asleep or unconscious. Her face was flushed with fever. Sally looked up as Melinda entered.

"I don't know what's happening," she said. "I'm so sick. I feel like I'm going to die."

"It's Frederick's ghost," Melinda said. "He's doing this to you. Kevin and Jim are sick, too. Stay here. I'll deal with the ghost. Once he's crossed over, this should end."

"April . . . how is she?"

"Sleeping," Melinda said.

"I'm so thirsty," Sally said. "But I can't get up."

Melinda hurried away and found the third-floor bathroom. Tools were scattered around the toilet, but the sink worked and a stack of plastic cups sat nearby. Melinda filled four of them with water. She held one for Sally, who drained it and almost instantly fell asleep. April wouldn't wake up for any.

Melinda left the cup within reach and, feeling like a nurse, brought the other two down the hall to Kevin and Jim, who took them gratefully.

"I should get you out of here," Melinda said as Jim drank. "Drive you to a hospital."

Jim shook his head and lay back. Some of the red spots were turning into pustules, marring his handsome face. "No. This isn't a normal disease. It's supernatural. Do you really think conventional medicine will help?"

Melinda bit her lip. "No."

"I didn't think so. And what if we gave it to someone else? What if it spread?"

Melinda hadn't thought of that. Leave it to Jim to think of other patients even as he lay sick and dy—

No. He wasn't. He wouldn't. No one was going to die.

"I'll be back," she said. Melinda marched out of the room and down the stairs. The second-floor hallway looked bleak and dismal. The shattered plaster on the walls and gritty piles of it on the floor made everything seem lost and broken beyond repair. Melinda firmly kept her fear and uncertainty in check as she stood at the threshold of the dusty plague room and faced the dry skeleton on the bed.

"I know you're here, Frederick," she said. "My name is Melinda Gordon. I'm here to help you. I want to hear your side."

A hard hand shoved her forward. Melinda fell into the room and hit the hard wooden floor. The door slammed behind her and the lock scraped shut. Melinda scrambled to her feet and flung herself at the door, but it was shut tight and the knob was gone. The room closed in around her like a coffin and she hammered at the door in blind panic for a moment, then forced herself to stop. She turned around and pressed her back to the wood, heart pounding, breath coming in gasps. Another sound thudded against her ears and thumped through her body. It was the steady *thock* of hammering. Someone was driving nails into the wood.

"No!" Melinda howled. "Stop it!"

The hammering continued. Every heavy *thock* and *thump* sealed her farther in. Melinda dashed for the window.

It wasn't there.

Melinda stood at the blank wall, dumbfounded. There was no sign that the window had ever existed. The hammering at the door continued. Melinda ran her hands over the wall as if she could find the window by touch, but all she felt was wallpaper. The only light in the room stole in from the crack under the door. She could barely see her hands as they scrabbled at the wall, searching desperately for the exit she knew had once been there.

Bones rattled. Cloth rustled and shadows shifted in the bed beside Melinda. A soft voice filled with ice spoke almost in her ear. *"You'll never leave this room, girl. You're all mine. You'll keep me company for a long, long—"*

Melinda punched it. The skeleton flew across the bed, hit the wall on the other side with a satisfying crack, and fell apart. The voice fell silent for a moment, then laughed again. With more rattles and clicks, the skeleton slid together. The teeth grinned yellow in the tiny slice of light that slid in. Frederick's skeleton cocked its head within its red-striped pajamas and gave Melinda an empty look. Melinda refused to flinch.

"You can't hurt a ghost. You can't escape. You can't get help. You can't, you can't, you can't." The skeleton leaned forward and exhaled cold graveyard breath into Melinda's face. *"You can't cross me over, you can't cure your husband, you can't help my pitiful descendants."*

Melinda held her ground. "Why do you want to hurt them? Florence is dead. Arthur's gone. Kevin and his family haven't done anything to you. They didn't even know."

"THIS IS MY HOUSE!" Frederick roared. *"They stole it from me, and I want it back."* A thin finger reached out and touched Melinda's cheek. She batted it away and Frederick snickered. *"Once your*

husband and my dear descendants are dead, you and I can live here forever."

Melinda clenched her teeth and forced the image of Jim's disease-riddled corpse from her mind. "Why me? Why do you want me?"

"You can see me. You can talk to me. I spent over eighty years in this room, and I'm . . . hungry."

"Not going to happen," Melinda said.

"Maybe I just need to persuade you a little more."

The last scrap of light vanished. Absolute blackness closed in around Melinda like the wings of a raven. She stood motionless, the sound of her own breathing in her ears. After a moment, tiny scritching sounds skittered behind her. Slowly she turned, though it made no difference. It was like standing in a pool of ink.

"Stop this," she said. "I won't—"

And then the fear smashed her to the floor. All her joints went as weak as water. Her heart beat so fast it hurt and her stomach tightened around a lump harder than a fist. Things in the dark were coming for her, reaching for her with long, cold claws. They clicked their teeth and licked dripping jowls. She could feel them coming for her. She wanted to run, but there was nowhere to run to, and the fear paralyzed every fiber. She couldn't move, couldn't react, couldn't think. Terror was a mountain pressing her down, squeezing the air from her lungs.

"You'll stay here forever, girl. You'll stay and talk to me."

Melinda reached out with one hand and touched the iron bedstead to orient herself. It was as cold as a bar of ice. She could feel the blood in her hand turn cold and run down her arm like a river of slush, but at least she knew where she was. Her heart continued to hammer. *There's nothing to be scared of,* she told herself. *This is the ghost's fear, not yours.* The fear didn't lessen one bit. She managed to crawl around until she was facing the door.

Tiny red lights glowed in the darkness just ahead of her. Eyes. They were eyes. Dozens of them. They stared at her, blinking just often enough to make it clear they were alive and hungry. Claws scratched the floor. Melinda's mouth went dry. The little red eyes were between her and the door.

They can't hurt you, she thought. *They can't do anything to you. Get up! Go!*

But her body wouldn't obey. She lay on the floor, unable to go forward or back. A tear squeezed out of the corner of her eye and ran down her cheek like a warm worm.

"Just the two of us. Forever."

And then the door screeched open. A bar of light flooded the room. The eyes vanished. Melinda looked up with a gasp. Standing in the doorway was a little girl. She wore jeans and a T-shirt, and two white cords ran from her ears to her pocket.

"April!" Melinda gasped.

"Come on, Melinda!" April said. *"You can do it! You can get out!"*

Melinda closed her eyes and choked on a sob. Sorrow crushed her worse than the fear. It was too much. April had died. The plague room had killed her, and it was Melinda's fault for letting Frederick out.

"Hurry, Melinda!" April's ghost called from the door. *"Come on! You can't die, too."*

"Shut up!" Frederick snarled behind her. *"Act like a lady!"*

"Who are you talking to?" Melinda managed. "Her or me?"

Frederick didn't answer. Melinda focused her gaze on April. Frederick had killed her. He had somehow infected her with smallpox, and now she was dead. A flicker of anger flared like a match scratched on a closet floor. It burned away some of the fear, and Melinda found she could move. She kept her eyes locked on April and crawled toward the door.

"No!" Frederick howled behind her. *"No! You will stay with me!"*

The distance between Melinda and the door lengthened. April slid backward until she was a dot in the distance. The room was a hundred yards long. Melinda tried to get to her feet, but the floorboards stretched and wobbled like taffy beneath her, hindering every movement.

"You'll never be able to leave," Frederick hissed.

Melinda looked at the impossible expanse of floor. She was trapped in a nightmare with no way out.

"Melinda! Hurry!" April called. Her voice was clear despite the apparent distance. *"You have to get out. Jim needs you! He's sick and he needs you!"*

The anger returned, flaring brighter than any match this time. Jim. How could she have forgotten about Jim for even a moment? She focused on April's distant figure and remembered Jim lying sick in a strange bed, sick because of this horrible ghost. Jim needed her. April needed her.

Without a backward glance, Melinda stormed to her feet and moved forward. Frederick screeched behind her, but Melinda ignored him. Phantom fingers dragged at her, but they didn't slow her down. She kept her eyes on April's tiny figure, newly dead because of Frederick—yes, because of *Frederick,* not Melinda. Frederick had chosen to infect her with smallpox; Frederick had killed her. Melinda had been involved, but it was Frederick who'd made the decision, Frederick who was at fault. Melinda's anger grew stronger with every step. The room abruptly shortened, and Melinda found herself at the door.

"Come on!" April said. *"Come out!"*

"No!" Frederick howled.

Melinda stepped across the threshold. Frederick's shrieks abruptly ended. Melinda found herself back in the perfectly normal hallway with its cracked plaster and piles of wainscoting on the floor, April standing a few paces away. Melinda gave a heavy sigh and allowed herself to lean against one of the walls for a moment with her eyes shut. But only for a moment—April would need help crossing over.

It never stops, she thought.

Melinda hated crossing children for the simple reason that it meant a child had died. A child's death was the height of unfairness, absolute proof that the universe could be cruel and detatched. A child's death was harder on the survivors than the death of an elder, and children were often reluctant to cross over. Adults saw their parents in the Light and wanted to go. Children saw their parents in the living world and needed to stay. What would she say to April? And then there was the problem of Jim and the surviving Rays being sick.

"Melinda?"

The voice was different. Melinda opened her eyes. Florence stood before her in the hallway. She still wore her faded housedress and tennis shoes, though her face wasn't quite as wrinkled and her cane was nowhere in sight. At her feet lay April, collapsed on the floor. No. It wasn't April. It was the puppet, April Too.

Melinda tried to speak, failed, tried again. "What?" she squeaked.

"*Hm!*" Florence said. "*I told you there was one more thing I needed to do before I left, sweetie.*"

"That was *you*?" Melinda said, still reeling.

"*I didn't think you'd overcome Father if it was me in the doorway, sweetie, so I borrowed the puppet here. I always did like dolls.*" She leaned over, picked up the puppet, and made it dance. "*Arthur made puppetry look like so much fun, though he took it a little far when he got out the scissors and attacked you. I'm sure he'd say he was sorry if he were here.*"

"Is April all right?"

"*She was sleeping when I got the puppet, but things may have changed.*" Florence released April Too and it dropped to the floor with a felty *thump.* "*Hm! That takes a lot out of a woman. And now I really do have to go. The Light is so amazing, I can't stay away anymore. Good-bye, sweetie. I'm sure you'll think of something to do with Father. Check on April for me.*"

With that, Florence turned and walked down the hallway, fading as she went.

"Thank you," Melinda called. The old woman turned and gave her a brief wave, then vanished forever.

11

MELINDA RAN UPSTAIRS with April Too in her arms. As she passed, she glanced into the room where Jim and Kevin were resting. Both men seemed to be asleep, and Melinda didn't stop. Much as she wanted to check on Jim, April might need her more.

Sally and April lay on the couch and love seat in the sitting room as before. Both were asleep. Boils and sores covered every inch of exposed skin. Masks of pustules hid their faces. Sally tossed restlessly, muttering in a fever dream. April appeared to be nearly comatose beneath her blanket, but she was breathing. Alive. Melinda stood over her, feeling helpless. Now that she was here, she realized she had no idea what to do. Jim was right—no doctor or medicine would be able to treat this disease, and if it were contagious, bringing April or any of the others to a hospital might start an epidemic. At least all of them were still alive. But for how long?

Melinda set April Too on a chair. Not for the first time, she wondered how spirits got objects from one place to another without anyone noticing. Did they somehow vanish from one place and reappear at another? Or did ghosts sneak them around when no one was looking?

She shook her head. Stupid, idle thoughts. She had more important problems to solve. The difficulty was, Melinda had no idea what to do next. Frederick wasn't listening to her, was actively trying to harm her. There was clearly no way to convince him to cross over. He was one of those few ghosts who simply wouldn't go, probably ever.

"Just because you got out of the sick room doesn't mean you escaped me."

Melinda spun. Frederick Ray stood framed in the doorway, dressed in his striped silk pajamas. Pustules covered his face and hands. Some of the sores had burst, and yellow fluid oozed out of them. Even as Melinda watched, another one broke open. A smell of rotting meat followed him, and Melinda gagged.

"Leave me alone," Melinda said. "Leave *them* alone. They haven't done anything to you."

"They're in my house." He lurched into the room. Melinda forced herself to stand her ground, but he went around her and leaned over April instead.

"She looks like Florence did as a child. So young. She makes me stronger and stronger. When she dies, I'll be strong enough to leave this house."

A chill ran down Melinda's back. "Why would you want to do that?" she asked, trying to stay casual. "This is your house. You said so."

"People are living on my land," Frederick said. *"Land I bought with my money, land they stole from me. It's mine, and I want it back."* He put out a pustule-coated finger to touch April's forehead, but it went through her. She whimpered in her sleep. *"I'll make them sick, too. I can take the plague with me wherever I go. Their sickness makes me stronger. They'll die and leave my land. All except you. You can see me, so you'll stay here to talk to me. Keep me company."*

"No," Melinda said. "I won't. There's nothing you can do to keep me here."

"I doubt that. There's your husband, after all." The ghost straightened and turned to face her. *"Obey me, and I'll let him live."*

Obey. Melinda remembered the man who had forced a clerk to eat dog food.

"You're lying," she said.

"Then watch him die, and when people come to take his body away, those people will die, too."

"You know that. You don't have the ability."

Frederick laughed. *"It doesn't matter. I can make them believe it. They will weaken and then they will die. They all will."*

Melinda turned on her heel and fled the room. Frederick's icy laugh followed her, but the ghost himself remained behind. She raced down the hall to the bedroom where Kevin and Jim lay huddled on their bare mattresses beneath borrowed blankets. Kevin was asleep or unconscious, she wasn't sure which, but Jim was awake. His eyes were bright with fever and his handsome face was heavily blistered. It twisted Melinda's heart to see him that way, and she was half ready to run back to Frederick's ghost, promise him anything to rid Jim of this disease.

"How do you feel?" she asked softly.

"Like I've been hit . . . by a freight train," he rasped. "Is it really . . . the ghost . . . doing this?"

Melinda knelt next to the bed and took his hand, ignoring the blisters. The palm was hot and dry. "I can't get him to cross over. He wants his house and lands back, and he's willing to start a plague to do it. He's feeding off your pain, which makes it easier for him to make other people sick. He'll never leave, Jim. I don't know what to do. I'm out of options."

"I can think . . . of one."

Melinda's heart leaped. "What? What is it?"

"Call . . . Wendy."

"No." The word popped out of Melinda's mouth before she even thought.

"Could she . . . get rid of the ghost?" Jim whispered.

"I don't know. Possibly." Melinda swallowed. "Jim, she does more harm than good. She never listens to anything I say. I get angry whenever I see her. How can I call her for help?"

"How is she . . . different . . . from a stubborn ghost?" Jim countered. His eyelids fluttered closed. "How is she different from . . . the mittens lady? Maybe you need to treat her . . . like a ghost . . . convince her . . . cross over . . . to your side." He fell unconscious.

Melinda's insides twisted as she knelt beside him, his blistered hand still in hers. Seeing him like this made her feel like a rock had fallen on her. When she and Jim had first gotten engaged, she had fantasized about taking care of him when he was sick. After all, a major illness was about the only time Melinda wanted someone to take care of *her*. When she got sick as a child, it was one of the few moments Mom turned tender and soft-hearted, making Melinda feel cozy and cared for. Melinda had been looking forward to giving Jim the same feeling. She would bring him soup and medicine and put the TV on for him and make sure the house stayed quiet until he felt better. But the first time Jim caught the flu, he turned into a wounded bear. He growled whenever Melinda came near him, no matter how nice she tried to be or what she offered to do for him. In the end, she set trays of food and medicine down for him while he slept and tiptoed away. Later, when Melinda came down with the same bug, Jim vacated the house and left her completely alone, which made her feel abandoned and upset. Later they had talked about it and Melinda had learned that Jim mostly wanted to be left alone when he was sick and he had assumed Melinda would want the same treatment, just as Melinda had assumed Jim would want to be coddled. Both had been surprised at the other, and eventually they had laughed about it. Now when Melinda got sick, Jim fluffed her pillows and brought soup, and when Jim got sick, Melinda stayed out of his way.

This, however, was different. This wasn't chicken soup and extra blankets and a favorite DVD. Jim was dying, and it was partly her fault. Frederick wanted to keep Melinda nearby because she could talk to him. She shuddered, feeling stupid and helpless.

Then why are you standing here? she thought, releasing Jim's hand. *You have a perfectly good solution at hand. Why don't you use it?*

Because it was Wendy. The thought of bringing her into this made Melinda clench both fists until the nails cut into her palms. Her condescending smile, her superior attitude, her smug looks.

Then she looked down at Jim. It was pride, pure and simple. Wendy might be able to handle this. How could she even consider letting pride get in the way of saving the lives of her husband and the Ray family?

Melinda remembered that Kevin had put Wendy's card in his shirt pocket. She crossed the room and gently slid her hand under the blankets. The shirt beneath was damp with sweat—or maybe something else. Melinda didn't want to think about that. Kevin didn't stir. His fever-flushed skin was nearly as red as his hair, and one of the pustules on his face leaked fluid. Melinda gritted her teeth and felt carefully around until she found the pocket and extracted the card within. Then she pulled her cell phone from her own pocket and, before she could lose her nerve, dialed the number. Wendy picked up on the second ring.

"It's Melinda." Even under these circumstances, she couldn't bring herself to use anything more polite than a clipped, icy voice. "I'm at the Ray house, and I think you need to come out here."

There was a brief pause. "Are you saying you need my help with a visitor?"

Melinda's hand tightened around the phone. It cost everything she had to say, "Yes."

"So I should bring my materials?"

"Yes. You should."

"You do know my services don't come cheaply."

Melinda never wanted to hit something more in her entire life. But she kept her voice level. "I'm aware of that. Just come."

"I think I can fit you in on Tuesday afternoon. Say, three o'clock?"

Melinda hadn't thought it was possible to dislike Wendy more. She came within a hair of snapping the phone shut, plague or no plague. Instead, she said, "Wendy, you need to come out here now. It's a life-or-death emergency." She took a deep breath and added, "Please."

A slight pause followed. "Since you asked so nicely, I'll be glad to help. Give me ten minutes." The connection ended.

Something made Melinda turn and look at Jim. His eyes were open again.

"She's coming," Melinda said.

"Good job," he said. "You did good, Mel."

Suddenly the thought of him being in this awful house was more than Melinda could bear. "Jim, we have to get you out of this place. Come on! Can you walk?"

She expected him to refuse, but he seemed to want to leave, as well. He managed to sit up with the blankets wrapped around him. Melinda helped him stand, then let him lean on her as he shuffled to the door. Even though it was clear he was trying not to put too much weight on her, his body was heavy and ungainly, and Melinda had a sudden fear that he would collapse on the floor and she wouldn't be able to move him. Maybe this wasn't such a good idea. But he was moving with some determination, and she decided to keep going. They got him to the stairs and down to the second-floor landing. Frederick appeared in front of them. His pox-ridden face clashed with his silk pajamas.

"Going somewhere?" he hissed.

Melinda ignored him. Jim couldn't see him, but his footsteps faltered as he rounded the bend in the stairs to head for the first floor.

"You can take him out of the house, but it won't cure him," Frederick said. *"He's trapped in the disease like the disease trapped me in that room."*

Melinda guided Jim down the stairs. Frederick gave a wet snort and vanished. Jim was breathing hard now, wheezing a little, and he was staggering. Melinda wondered if she was strong enough to carry April out of the house, too.

They made it as far as the front parlor before Jim's knees gave way. "I can't," he gasped. "I can't."

Melinda whipped the dust cover off a high-backed sofa and Jim collapsed onto it. She bundled the blankets around his shivering body.

"I'm sorry," he rasped. "I just can't walk."

"You don't have anything to be sorry about," Melinda said. "Oh God—Jim, you hold on. You—"

"Yoo-hoo!" Wendy King, dressed in her gray suit with her duffel bag slung over her shoulder, stood in the doorway. "You said you needed help, Melinda, and I am here. I hope you don't mind that I came in without knocking."

To Melinda's surprise, her first emotion was a bit of gladness. Here was another ally, however unpleasant. Someone who would understand and who could help. Wendy, the bitch queen of ghosts, would stomp all over Frederick Ray.

"My God," Wendy said. "What's wrong with your husband?"

"Supernatural smallpox," Melinda said, and swiftly explained what had happened. Jim slept on the sofa, and Melinda had to work at keeping her voice level.

"So sending one visitor into the Light freed another, more malevolent one," Wendy said thoughtfully. "Oh, dear."

"Yeah. Something you never thought to consider when you bludgeoned Arthur into the hereafter."

"Well, I am here now," Wendy said briskly. "And since this seems to be at least partly my fault, I suppose I should give a discount on my fee."

"*Partly* your fault?" Melinda squawked. "A *discount*?"

"It's against good business principles, but—"

Melinda stepped forward and thrust a finger into Wendy's face. "Think of it this way—you want to go into business in Grandview, right? If you don't get rid of Frederick Ray, he's going to unleash a plague that will wipe out most of the town. That will include all your potential customers and *you*. In fact, you might be getting sick even as we speak.

Feeling feverish? A little achy? I think you should get to work, and fast."

"No need to get snippy," Wendy replied in that calm voice Melinda had begun to hate. Did the woman have no emotions? "I guess this once I can offer my services gratis." She gave a stony smile and turned for the staircase. "Just don't tell my accountant."

"Was that a joke?" Melinda asked in disbelief. "Did you just tell a joke?"

But Wendy was already going upstairs. Melinda paused long enough to kiss the top of Jim's head before following.

On the second floor, Melinda showed Wendy to the plague room. Wendy peered inside with pursed lips. "I've heard of such places, though I've never encountered one. I can see why the visitor might be angry."

Melinda was keeping a wary eye out for Frederick, but didn't see him anywhere, unless you counted the grisly skeleton still lying on the bed. "There's more to the situation than that," she said, "but it'll do for now. Can you handle it?"

"Of course. I am strong. I have a one hundred percent success rate."

Melinda didn't comment.

The table Wendy had used before was still standing at the far end of the hallway. Melinda watched with one eye as Wendy set up her paraphernalia and used the other eye as lookout for Frederick. Still no sign of him. Melinda dashed upstairs to check on the Rays. All three of them were deeply asleep, and Melinda was unable to rouse any of them. Clearly, they were getting worse. Little April's lips were cracked, her face was a mass of sores. Frederick was nowhere to be seen.

On the table just outside the plague room, Wendy put out her bowl on its red silk cushion, the wooden mallet, the skull, the book, new candles, the incense burner, and the silver knife. Her movements were practiced and precise. Melinda fidgeted from her position a few feet away.

"Anything I can do to help?" she asked.

"No," Wendy said. "Just stay back."

The ghost of Wendy's father came into existence behind her. His features were still blurred, though Melinda could make out his beard and receding hairline. He brushed a hand over Wendy's shoulder.

"Your father's here," Melinda said.

"I know." She lit the candles and the incense, then waved the aromatic smoke around with her hand. "I cleanse this place and make it mine."

Tiny green sparks crackled along the table and danced over the floor. The air seemed to gather and thicken. Melinda's mind was going in a hundred different directions—worrying about Jim and the Rays, wondering where Frederick was and when he'd turn up, feeling like a helpless bystander when she was usually involved in getting things done.

"What do the sparks do?" Melinda asked to take her mind off her worries more than anything else.

"What sparks?" Wendy said, opening the book to a well-worn page.

"Never mind."

Wendy continued her methodical work. She reminded Melinda of a chef making a recipe from memory. Her face was calm, her movements firm and competent. Her father watched silently behind her, ignoring Melinda completely. Melinda was surprised to feel a certain amount of relief. Wendy seemed to know exactly what she was doing and did it with ease of long practice. Melinda began to see why her . . . customers trusted her. She radiated calm for people whose lives had been turned inside out by spirits. It was too bad her methods were ultimately terrible.

Now Melinda was advocating them, but she didn't see much choice. Frederick had made it clear he wasn't going to cross over, and that he was going to kill innocent people as long as he remained in this world. Much as Melinda loathed the idea of causing anyone pain, she wasn't going to let Frederick kill anyone or spread his filthy disease to an unsuspecting Grandview. Melinda wondered if she would feel Frederick's pain when Wendy yanked him into the Light. She had felt the pain of the other spirits Wendy had crossed over, after all. Melinda shuddered at the idea, then thought of Jim, and her resolve stiffened. If it meant Jim getting better, she would do it a hundred times over and feel it a thousand times worse.

"I'm ready," Wendy said. "Stay back and don't interfere, no matter what you see or hear."

Melinda crossed her arms and leaned against a cracked wall, trying to look nonchalant when her husband was dying only a few yards away. She wanted to grab Wendy and force her to hurry, shout at her to *move*, dammit! "Got it."

Wendy waved more incense with her hand and started a low chant Melinda couldn't make out. She swayed back and forth and made beckoning gestures. More green sparks leaped and snapped from the objects on the table. They jumped into the air like tiny fireflies. The chant continued, droned louder. It was in a language Melinda didn't recognize. Small shards of green and blue lighting arced from the table to the walls with ear-popping crackling sounds, and Melinda wondered how Wendy couldn't see or hear them. Behind Wendy, her father's spirit stood motionless, watchful as a soldier.

Wendy's eyes glazed over and she moved her hand. Her father moved his hand as well, keeping it just above hers. Wendy picked up the mallet and lightly struck the bronze bowl, her father following along. The sound boomed through the house, thudding against Melinda's bones, and she clapped her hands over her ears. Wendy didn't seem to notice.

"I call the visitor who haunts this place," Wendy intoned. "I summon you to stand before me." She and her father struck the bowl again, louder this time. Melinda kept her hands pressed against her ears, but it was like standing next to a church bell. The floor vibrated and bits of plaster fell from the cracked walls.

"I summon you to stand before me *now*," Wendy boomed. Woman and spirit struck the bowl once more, and the sound drove Melinda to her knees. More plaster dropped from the walls and the floor seemed to rock beneath her.

A hot breeze rose and blew down the corridor. It stirred the heavy blue smoke drifting from the incense burner but left the candles undisturbed. Melinda cautiously took her hands away from her ears just as Frederick rushed down the hall from nowhere. His plague-ravaged face oozed pinkish yellow fluids. Spittle flew from his snarling mouth. He lunged at Wendy. *"Get out of my house!"*

Melinda automatically reached for Wendy, though she was too far away to do anything. Wendy's father was faster. He appeared between Wendy and Frederick and made the "stop" gesture Melinda had seen him make before when Arthur had tried to attack. Unlike Arthur, however, Frederick didn't even pause. He stiff-armed Wendy's father, a palm punch that slammed his chest. A blurry look of shock and surprise crossed the other spirit's face before the blow knocked him backward, through the table, and into the wall. He vanished.

12

"Oh!" Wendy said. Two of her candles went out.

"Look out!" Melinda shouted.

"My house!" Frederick howled. He slashed both hands through Wendy's torso like daggers. Wendy choked and staggered backward, clutching her chest. Melinda leaped forward and grabbed her arm. The breeze turned into a wind that whipped their clothes and tore at their hair. Book pages fluttered and flapped and the skull rolled off the table.

"Come on!" Melinda shouted. She hauled Wendy toward the stairs.

"What's happening?" Wendy screamed above the noise of the wind.

"Get out of my house!" Frederick screeched behind them. Glass shattered somewhere and wood creaked as if the beams were protesting. The wind continued to blast at them. Sawdust and bits of

plaster scoured Melinda's skin and threw grit into her eyes. She and Wendy had to squint in order to see and were forced to make their way down the steps mostly by feel. They managed to get down to the first floor, but the wind didn't slow. Wendy moved toward the door.

"We have to get out of here!" she yelled.

"Jim!" Melinda shouted. "He's still in the parlor!"

Melinda half expected Wendy to say they should leave him, but the other woman altered course without comment and forced her way with Melinda into the parlor. The place was chaos. Freed of the furniture, dust covers flapped and whipped around the room like Halloween ghosts. Dust and grit filled the air. Jim lay huddled beneath his blankets on the sofa, his face hidden. The two women staggered toward him and Melinda laid a hand on his shoulder. He jumped. Melinda pulled the blanket away from his face so he could see it was her. He looked both relieved and frightened.

"Don't try to talk," she yelled over the noise. "We've got to get you out! Wendy's going to help!"

The two of them got Jim to his feet, still wrapped in blankets. Melinda noticed that most of his sores were oozing and he was barely able to walk. Somehow, they got him to the front door. It opened at Melinda's touch. The wind blew them out onto the porch, then abruptly ceased as the door slammed shut behind them. The silence rang in Melinda's ears. Clouds had moved in, gray and heavy as cement, and a damp autumn chill had invaded the air. Jim swayed on his feet, clearly at the end of his strength, and Melinda feared he would drop before they could get him somewhere safe.

"What the hell happened?" Wendy said. Her face was as gray as her clothes.

"Come on, Jim," Melinda said. "Let's get you into the truck."

Jim didn't respond. Instead, he let Melinda and Wendy help him down the overgrown walkway. The daylilies were dying, and their tendrils reached out like brown fingers to caress their legs as they passed. Melinda threw a glance over her shoulder at the tall, spiky house. Against the concrete clouds, the faded red walls looked almost bloody. The third-floor windows looked out over nothing. The Rays were still up there, dying, giving up their life energy to the spirit of a malevolent ancestor, a man who would use their energy to spread death and destruction farther than any spirit Melinda had ever encountered.

Jim made it to the SUV and all but fell into the rear seat. He still hadn't spoken. Melinda breathed a small sigh of relief. A thought struck her—she could drive Jim to a doctor or even the hospital. Would she do that on the slim chance they could help him, even if it meant risking the lives of other people? Tears born of anger and frustration welled up. Dammit, why was she put into this position? Why did *she* have to decide? She touched Jim's shoulder and gently closed the truck door. Wendy was standing on the broken driveway behind her, her face set and hard. It was an expression Melinda had never seen her wear before.

"That's never happened to me before," Wendy said in a dangerous voice. "Not ever. That . . . *thing* touched me. I felt it go through me like a knife made of ice. It grabbed my heart for a moment and almost made it stop."

Melinda's own anger rose, and a sharp retort came to the tip of her tongue, one that would remind Wendy that all spirits, no matter how malevolent, were people, not things. But Jim's presence in the truck behind her made her think of what he had said earlier. Why treat Wendy any different from an angry spirit?

You learn more by listening than speaking, Grandma had always said. Listen, listen, and listen some more.

"You're angry," Melinda prompted.

"You're damn right I'm angry," Wendy exploded. "I have a *right* to be angry after all that."

"It's more than that, though, isn't it?" Melinda said. An inner voice yammered at her, urging her to hurry, move, *do* something besides talk. But she forced herself to look relaxed, even lean against the cool metal of the red SUV. "It's not just ghosts."

"It's *always* ghosts!" Wendy exploded. "It's my whole life!" She began to pace up and down the driveway beside the truck. "Everything I do is ghosts, ghosts, ghosts! Control the ghosts, be strong and control the ghosts. And now look what happened to me—to *them.* People are sick in there and dying because I wasn't strong enough. Shit!"

Melinda was so startled at hearing Wendy swear that she almost didn't notice Wendy's father appear behind her. He was sharper now, his features clear. He had a hooked nose and heavy eyebrows, a strong jaw, and acne-pitted skin. Both beard and the remains of his hair were iron gray. He wore a tweed jacket with patches on the elbows, a collared shirt, and a worn-looking green tie.

"I agree," he said. *"She's weak. No matter how hard I taught her to be strong, she never quite made it."*

"They're dying because you weren't strong enough?" Melinda echoed, ignoring Wendy's father for the moment.

"Yes." The word came out as a hiss. "You have to be strong in this business, or the spirits can overpower you. I'm sure you, of all people, know that. You're never allowed a moment of weakness, and now . . ."

"You had such a moment in the house?" Melinda hazarded.

Some of Wendy's anger seemed to crumple. "I did. God. All I could think about was what happened to your husband and to the Rays. It was enough to shake my concentration, and . . . well, you saw what happened."

"*Weak,*" her father repeated.

"Human," Melinda corrected.

"What?" Wendy said.

"You're human," Melinda said. "Look, no one can be strong every moment of their lives."

"*With that attitude, no wonder you're a failure,*" Wendy's father said to her. "*Just like my daughter.*"

"You have to be in this game," Wendy replied.

"How does it work for you?" Melinda asked. "Do you really need all the paraphernalia? The book and skull and the bowl?"

"They help, but they aren't necessary," Wendy admitted. "They help me focus my mind and set the mood, both for myself and the clients. Ultimately, it boils down to a battle of willpower between me and the vis—the ghost. Whoever is stronger wins, and I. Always. Win."

"*Because I help her,*" Wendy's father put in. "*She's weak on her own. Never could do anything by herself.*"

"I would appreciate it if you kept the remarks to youself," Melinda snapped.

Wendy blinked. "What? Who are you—oh. He's here, isn't he?"

"*Always. She needs me.*"

"He's behind you."

"He's always been behind me," Wendy said. "Our family has a gift. We've been mediums and spiritualists for generations, crossing stubborn spirits over to help the living get on with their lives. Dad showed me the family business, but he never let me go. He never let me do anything on my own because he said I wasn't strong enough."

"She isn't. She was always weak. Just like her mother. The smallest thing made her cry when she was a child."

"My grandmother had me talking to spirits and the survivors on my own when I was very young," Melinda said. "The first time was when I was eight or nine. We were at a funeral. The ghost of the departed had a final message he needed to give his wife, and Grandma made me give it to her on my own."

"Dad never did that to me," Wendy said. "I've never done it on my own."

"She can't be trusted with it," her father said.

"Have you talked to him about this?"

Wendy made a scornful noise. "That's not the way it works. Spirits can be sensed, not seen. You can talk to them a little if they're willing to make noises—rap once for yes and twice for no, that sort of thing, but that makes true conversation difficult."

"I talk to them all the time," Melinda said.

"Yes, that's what you've said. Showmanship is an important part of this job, and I gave you points for that, but frankly, I know better."

Ah. Melinda had been down the "I don't believe you" road a hundred times. Feeling on firmer ground, she said, "Do you want to talk to your father now?"

"Don't try the show with me," Wendy said. "Not now. We have other problems."

Melinda turned to the ghost, acutely aware that her husband was sick in the truck behind her, but having to go through the motions of this. "What's your first name, Mr. King?"

"Why should I tell you?" he countered.

"I'm trying to sort all this out so we can deal with Frederick Ray, and I can't do it until both of you are convinced of what I can do."

"All right. It's Norman."

"Hello, Norman. I'm Melinda."

"A nice trick," Wendy said. "Internet database? Did you look up my birth certificate? I know he's there, mind you—I just don't believe you can talk to him."

"Let's do this fast, then," Melinda said. "I don't want to take up more time. Jim is sick and the Rays are dying. Norman, tell me something about Wendy that I couldn't possibly know."

A hard smile crossed Norman's face. *"My daughter always has to be right. Fine, then. When Wendy was sixteen, she went to the waterpark with some friends, including a boy she had a crush on. I believe his name was Ryan. She went down one of the slides and when she hit the pool at the bottom, the top of her bathing suit came off and floated away. She didn't notice right away and stood up—right in front of the boy she liked."*

Melinda put her hands to her mouth. "Oh, no!"

"It turned out that one of her so-called friends had a camera handy and snapped a picture. The print circulated around school, and she was known as Topless Wendy all year."

Melinda felt her face begin to heat up with embarrassment on Wendy's behalf. Before she could say anything, Norman continued.

"Young Ryan got hold of the picture and apparently decided that Wendy had flashed him on purpose. One day after school, he cornered her alone in a classroom and groped her extensively before she got away. She came home in tears and told me about it."

"What did you do?" Melinda asked, shocked.

"Nothing. If she wasn't strong enough to handle it, the incident would teach her to be. She let him do it to her, after all."

More outrage swept over Melinda. "You stood by and did *nothing*? She's your daughter!"

"What are you talking about?" Wendy demanded.

"He told me the Topless Wendy story," Melinda said. "And he told me what Ryan did to you afterward."

Wendy's face went white. "He didn't."

"I'm afraid so," Melinda said. "Look—"

"That was the worst year of my life, you bastard," Wendy said to the empty air. "I still have nightmares about him in the classroom. I had to sit next to him in class the next day and endure him looking at me, making little remarks when the teacher couldn't hear. I was too scared to tell anyone else after you didn't do anything to help."

"I shouldn't have had to help," Norman retorted. *"You needed to be strong and help yourself."*

"He says you should have been strong on your own," Melinda said. She shot a nervous glance at the thin spires of the Ray house.

"Oh, sure," Wendy said. Her anger was growing, like a sandstorm whirling closer across the dunes. "That's your answer to everything. If I'm supposed to be so strong, Dad, then why haven't you left me alone?"

"You aren't strong enough to handle spirits on your own."

"He says you can't handle ghosts by yourself," Melinda said.

"YOU NEVER LET ME!" Wendy shouted. "Every day, you made me prove I was strong, but you never once said I did it right. Never once!"

"Exorcism is a battle of wills," Norman said. *"You against the spirit. The weak can't win. You're weak! Today proved it!"*

Melinda relayed this, wincing as she did so. Wendy's face went stony. "Then maybe I should prove it now." She reached into her pocket and pulled out the silver knife.

"You don't have the strength or the will," Norman snorted, and Melinda relayed his words without thinking. *"You're already growing weaker."*

"Really, Dad? Really? I'm tired of you looking over my shoulder every minute." Wendy's voice dripped venom. "I'm thirty years old. I don't need you anymore. Maybe it's time to prove that."

"Wendy!" Melinda said in shock. "Look at your hands!"

Wendy glanced down. For a moment she didn't seem to understand what she was looking at. Then she screamed. A red rash was crawling over the backs of her hands. It stippled her face as well, and her skin was starting to flush with fever.

"No!" Wendy said. "No!"

"She's too weak to fight him off," Norman said in disgust. *"Maybe she'd be better off dead."*

"I heard that," Wendy shouted. "God, I actually heard you this time."

"Because you're getting closer to death, I imagine. Look at your rash. It's growing worse."

"You think I can't do it, Dad?" Wendy spun in place, facing him directly. It was clear she could see him now, and her knife was pointed at him, a glittering gray blade beneath a cloudy sky. "Let's see how weak I really am."

"Wendy, you don't want to do that," Melinda said suddenly. "Forced crossings—"

"No, Melinda—you were right. He's dead, and I need to move him out of my life. Permanently."

"I never said anything like that," Melinda protested.

"You didn't? Maybe that's what I've been telling myself, then, and I've finally started to listen."

Norman's face became set and hard. He looked a lot like his daughter. *I'm not leaving, Wendy.*

"Yes, Dad. You are."

Wendy began to chant. A chilly breeze stirred the long grass beside the driveway. Her knife gleamed like a star, and green lightning leaped from it to ground on the gravel. A silver thread spun itself from Norman's chest and wound through the air. It circled around Wendy, either anchoring her or binding her, Melinda couldn't tell.

A coughing spasm abruptly shook Wendy's body. The chant ended, the lightning vanished, the silver thread flickered and grew dim. The rash on her body was growing worse. Melinda stepped forward, but Wendy made a sharp gesture, ordering her back.

"Weak," Norman said. *"I'm not leaving you. You need me. You'll always need me."*

The coughing ended. Wendy wiped her mouth with the back of one hand, rash and all, and brandished the knife again. "I've never had a romantic relationship in my entire life. For years I told myself it's because of what Ryan did to me, but it's time to tell the truth. It's because of you."

She started chanting again, and the thread reappeared. Melinda kept her distance, falling into observer mode. It usually happened this way. She was the catalyst, the flicker that started the chain reaction. Once conversation actually got started between the living and the dead, Melinda often ended up with very little to do except observe. The other people had to sort things out for themselves. This case, however, was more extreme than most.

Melinda realized that this time Wendy could see the thread clearly. Perhaps Norman was right and it was because Wendy was closer to death or, Melinda thought more likely, Wendy had the ability to see it all along, but her dependence on her father as a spirit guide had interfered. Now she was letting herself go, using her power fully for the first time in her life.

Wendy's hands were shaking, and her face was ravaged with rash and fever. Her eyes were glazed with sickness or with power, Melinda couldn't tell which, but the chant rippled endlessly from her tongue. Norman's thread gleamed as bright as Wendy's knife. He stepped forward, his face still set as hard as stone.

"Stop it!" he barked. *"You will stop now!"*

"I release you!" Wendy howled. "I release you from this place! Go into the Light, shining one!"

She reached out with one spotted hand and grabbed a loop of the silver thread. Norman bellowed in outrage, and Melinda gasped sharply. His feelings of violation and disgust punched her in the gut, and she leaned heavily against the SUV. Inside, she could make out Jim's unconscious form.

"Jim . . ." she whispered.

"I release you!" Wendy shouted again. Wind swirled around her, pulling her hair free and whipping it around her head. She raised the knife and brought it down.

Norman caught her wrist. *"No!"*

The two stood frozen, unmoving as concrete statues. Then Wendy's arm came up, the knife slowly moving away from the thread. Wendy gritted her teeth. Her face was flushed so red the plague rash was barely visible. She was panting, gasping for air. Norman pulled steadily, inexorably.

"Let it go, girl," he hissed, and somehow his voice carried over the wind. *"You can't win this fight. You'll never be strong enough. You never were."*

Tears streamed down Wendy's face. "Do you love me, Dad?" she panted. "Tell me the truth."

Norman hesitated, and Melinda, feeling his emotions at that moment, knew it wasn't from surprise at the question. He simply didn't know the answer.

"That's what I thought." And with her free hand, Wendy yanked hard on Norman's silver thread. Pain lanced through Melinda's chest. It felt like someone was pulling her heart out, squeezing it through her rib cage. With an agonized wail, Norman let go of Wendy's wrist and went down to one knee. She stood over him, her long brown hair streaming in the wind. Her body weaved, her hands shook like frightened leaves, but her expression remained determined.

"Good-bye, Dad. I hope you're happier on the other side." And she slashed through the thread with the shining knife.

The pain nearly ripped Melinda in half, and she went to her knees. Norman let out a single, long wail. He clawed at the air, then gathered himself and leaped at Wendy. She flung up her hands in a defensive gesture. Then he vanished.

The pain abruptly ended as if it had never been. The air stilled. Melinda got cautiously to her feet. Wendy looked around, still weaving heavily on her feet and panting as if she had run a marathon.

"I did it," she said. "I really did it. I—oh! Oh . . . dear."

And she collapsed to the ground.

"Wendy!" Melinda knelt next to the other woman's motionless form and shook her. "Wendy!"

No response. Wendy lay facedown, half on the driveway, half on the grass. A sprinkle of cool rain scattered across the lawn like tiny tears, then ceased. Melinda rolled Wendy over. Her skin was a waxy pale between the plague sores, a complete change from her earlier feverish red. Melinda felt for a pulse at her neck with chilly fingers. Nothing. Melinda put an ear to Wendy's mouth and nose to check her breathing. Nothing. Wendy King was dead.

Melinda's throat choked up and tears leaked from her eyes. She scrubbed at them furiously, but they wouldn't go away. She couldn't sort it all out. It was too much, too fast. She had disliked Wendy intensely for so long and then learned more about her, learned what had made her what she was. Melinda's father had abandoned her, run off for unknown reasons when she was just a little girl, and the scars she bore ran as deep as unlit canyons. Wendy had the opposite problem, a father who wouldn't let go, and now that Melinda knew it, she found her dislike of Wendy dissolving into sympathy—just in time to watch her die. Melinda cried for her, cried for the crimes committed against her, cried for her as her father had never done.

At last the storm of tears subsided. Melinda sat back on her heels and looked from the gloomy Ray house to the SUV and back again. She ran to the SUV and opened the door. Jim was unconscious, and she couldn't rouse him. He was slipping further and further into the disease. No doubt the Rays were in the same condition. Wendy was dead. Melinda was completely alone. Her hands shook. She hadn't realized how much she had been hoping Wendy would be able to handle Frederick Ray's ghost until now.

Sometimes there just isn't anybody else, said Grandma's voice in her head. When that happens, there's no use putting it off.

Slowly, Melinda pushed herself to her feet and walked with determined steps toward the house of Frederick Ray.

13

Melinda couldn't bring herself to check on the Rays in case the worst had already happened. She simply couldn't face the possibility of staring down at the lifeless body of April Ray. Instead she forced herself to walk up the creaky wooden staircase to the second-floor corridor she now knew as well her own home. How long had it been since she had been home? It felt like years. If she ever returned there, she would find everything covered in cobwebs, with layers of dust thick enough to leave footprints.

If, she thought. *When did I start thinking* if *instead of* when?

Wendy's body still lay on the front lawn. Melinda didn't feel right about leaving it—her—there, but there was no time to call 911 and deal with the inevitable difficult explanations. The best solution she could think of was to dash outside with a dust cover from the parlor and draw it over Wendy's remains. Melinda had no idea how she would explain all this to the authorities if she managed to—

When, she admonished herself. *When you manage to deal with the ghost.*

But the thoughts weren't very convincing. Her heart beat faster with every step she took down the hated hallway, and her mouth was dry. She realized she was panting as she reached the doorway to the plague room. Inside, she could see the shrunken skeleton still lying on the plain iron bed. She stared at it for a long moment.

"Frederick?" Melinda said at last. "I know you can hear me. Listen to me, please. You've made your point. You're strong, stronger than anyone. You can do whatever you want to anybody. I'm asking you, even if you don't cross over, please end this disease. You're hurting innocent people who—"

A crushing force shoved her backward and slammed her against the wall opposite the plague room door. The air burst from her lungs. Her feet dangled above the threadbare runner. Then the force abruptly vanished and she dropped to the floor, landing on hands and knees. Dull, bruising pain pressed against her back.

"The land is mine," Frederick hissed in her ear. His breath was cold. *"And if you won't share it with me, you'll share* this *instead."*

A red rash crawled across Melinda's arms and hands. Fever chills came over her in waves and her teeth chattered. Her strength ebbed.

"No, Frederick," she said. A fit of coughing burst from her throat. "Don't do this. I can help you. I only want to help."

Frederick stood over her, arms folded, the stern father looking down at the troublesome daughter. His pustules soaked his pajamas with ichor, and the whites of his eyes were as yellow as old ivory. *"You* can *help. You make me stronger as you get weak. I'll add your strength to mine, and then—"*

"You'll leave this place. Shining one."

Melinda looked up. Wendy King was standing between her and Frederick. Her gray suit looked a little damp and her hair was down, just as it had been when she died. But her skin was free of smallpox.

"Wendy?" Melinda said.

"What are you doing in my house?" Frederick demanded. His tone was belligerent, but he had backed up a few steps, looking startled.

"Your little plague weakened me," Wendy said, *"and that fight with my father apparently finished it. So here I am, thanks to you. Poetic justice, I suppose."*

Wendy held out a hand to help Melinda up, though it was more a gesture of friendship than actual help. Melinda managed to get to her feet anyway.

"*I can't cross over,*" she said archly. "*There seems to be something I have left undone. Now what do you think it could be, dear?*"

Melinda had to smile in spite of herself. "Let me think a moment."

"*Can we do this?*" Wendy asked. She looked a little uncertain.

"*You can't be serious,*" Frederick growled. "*You couldn't face me in life, and now you think you have a chance after death?*"

The fear and uncertainly abruptly left Melinda. Confidence filled her, and she stepped forward to face Frederick side by side with Wendy. "Yes," she said. "I know what our mistake was, Frederick. First we worked against each other as rivals. Then we worked separately to solve this problem. But now . . ."

"*Now,*" Wendy said, "*we are together.*"

Frederick leaped for them both with an ear-splitting howl. Spittle flew from his mouth and his fingers hooked into claws. But Wendy stepped in front of Melinda and snapped out a hand in the exact same gesture her father had used. Frederick slammed to a stop as if he'd hit a slab of stone. He grunted and dropped to the floor.

"*So that's how it works,*" Wendy said. "*Dad was stealing energy from other spirits. That's how he was so strong. It wasn't anything intrinsic to him.*"

"Look out!" Melinda shouted.

Frederick swiped a hand at Wendy's leg. Wendy skipped back just in time and made a sharp palm-down gesture. Frederick slammed back to the floor. Wendy swayed. The fight was already taking a lot out of her.

"Frederick!" Melinda said. "Listen to me! We don't want to fight you. We will, but we don't want to. You can cross into the Light, and you won't have to worry about anything ever. You'll be happy there. Your wife, Regina, is there. She's waiting for you."

"Don't you mention her name!" Frederick screamed. *"You'll pay for saying her name!"*

A wave of fever chills ran down Melinda's body, and every bone and joint began to ache. It seemed like she could feel every molecule of air that struck her skin. The rash grew more intense and the floor swayed.

"Stop it, Frederick!" Wendy commanded. She began to chant. The now-familiar silver thread wound its way from Frederick's chest and into the plague room. Melinda saw it lead to the skeleton that lay on the bed. And several things clicked into place.

Dina's thread had been anchored to the recipe book hidden under the floor. Mr. Xing's thread had been anchored somewhere in his bedroom, probably to his desk and the card with the address in Hong Kong. Arthur's thread had been anchored to a point in the hallway, and now that Melinda thought about it, she realized that it was the exact spot where the plague room door had been hidden. Frederick's thread was anchored to his skeleton.

The grave is empty.

Frederick said he wanted land.

"You can't stop me with a little Indian chant, girl," Frederick snarled. *"I don't need to fight you. I have enough power to leave this house now. I'm going to spread my pox wherever I go."* He turned to slide through the wall.

"Stop him, Wendy!" Melinda said. "Don't let him go!"

Wendy snatched a loop of thread. It wound around her wrist. She gave a sharp tug. Frederick stiffened and halted. Melinda braced herself for the feeling of horror and violation, but it didn't come. Perhaps it was because the person touching the thread was a ghost or because Melinda was already feeling sick. Either way, Melinda wasn't going to question it.

"Let me go!" Frederick screeched. He rounded on Wendy, trying to claw at her, but Wendy gave the thread another sharp tug and he flinched in pain. *"Fine, then—cut it, if that's what you're going to do!"*

"I can't," Wendy said. *"Only a living person who's been trained in the techniques can do that."*

At that, Frederick laughed. *"Then we're at a standoff."*

"Bring him into the plague room," Melinda said.

"No! I'm not going back in there," Frederick screamed. *"Never again!"*

In answer, Wendy stepped into the little room and jerked hard on the thread. Frederick went to one knee in the doorway, his sores dripping on the floor. Melinda heard the cold tapping of the droplets as they touched old wood and vanished.

"No!" he gasped. *"I'll never stop trying to escape, girl. You'll have to stay in here with me forever."*

"If I have to," Wendy said grimly. *"It would be a fitting penance for all the pain I've caused."* She yanked on the thread again, and jerked Frederick into the room bit by painful bit. He fought and bit and snarled like a rabid dog, but he couldn't resist the pull. Once he was fully inside, Melinda followed him in and slammed the door.

"You're going to stay, too?" Frederick gasped. *"I find that hard to believe."*

A wave of nausea sloshed through Melinda's stomach and several of the spots on her hands changed into pustules before her eyes. She leaned heavily against the wall. Jim. She would stay on her feet for Jim.

"Listen to me, Frederick," Melinda said. "Please. Your immediate family has all crossed over. So have your friends. The only people left are ones you've never met. They're all strangers to you."

She coughed hard for several seconds. Now she knew what Jim meant when he said he felt like he'd been hit by a truck. Her whole body was one giant ache. Frederick laughed at her coughing fit, but Wendy jerked the thread and he fell silent.

"If you cross over," Melinda said, "I'll bury your bones in your grave on your land. You'll own it forever, be part of it forever."

"And if I don't?"

Melinda let a little anger out, but only enough to put a hint of steel into her voice. It was getting harder to remain standing. "Wendy will hold you here while I scatter your bones across a county where you never owned land at all. I think I can manage that before I get too much sicker. How powerful will you be then?"

Frederick stared at her for a long time through his horrific mask of sores while Wendy gripped his thread with unyielding fingers. Melinda held her breath.

Come on, she thought. *Come on, you old bastard.*

Frederick seemed to struggle internally. Melinda felt her knees begin to weaken, and she leaned against the wall in order to remain standing. At last, Frederick's horrific face crumpled in defeat.

"I don't know how," he wailed. *"I don't see a light. I don't know how to cross over."*

All the rage and belligerence left him. His knelt on the floor in his striped pajamas looking old and pitiful.

"Is there anything you feel you should do?" Melinda asked. "Something that you left undone?"

"I can't think of anything," Frederick replied, his voice sad. The emotion sounded strange coming from him.

"Is there anyone you want to talk to?" Melinda said. "Kevin? Or April? They're your descendants."

"Like you pointed out, I don't even know them. I don't know what to do. I'm trapped here forever."

Melinda cast her mind about. No tasks, no relatives, no friends. What was left? She looked at the silver thread that ran from Frederick to Wendy to the skeleton. Then she looked at the door, with its ancient bloodstains, and something else occurred to her. She summoned up the last of her fading strength, staggered over to the bed, and carefully gathered the blankets around the skeleton and its disintegrating striped pajamas. It made a light bundle, nothing so much as like a pile of sticks. The thread looped around Melinda, as if unwilling to go through her.

"What are you doing?" Wendy asked.

"Follow me," Melinda said, and took the sad bundle out into the hallway. Wendy followed, and Frederick came behind her. The moment Melinda cleared the threshold, Frederick let out a long, heavy sigh of pure relief.

"Yes," he whispered. *"Oh, yes. Farther! Farther out! Take me out!"*

Melinda felt better, stronger, with every step. She glanced down at her hands and saw the sores were receding. She glanced over her shoulder and saw Frederick's face was beginning to clear as well. The pustules had become a bad rash and the fever flush was draining from his face. Wendy watched with interest, but didn't lose her hold on Frederick's thread.

Down the creaking wooden steps, through the foyer. A brief pause while Melinda figured out how to open the front door without putting down the blanketed bundle. Fresh autumn air flooded her lungs with new life. Frederick stepped up beside her. His face was almost completely clear, and Melinda could now see the man from Florence's past. He was rather handsome, made more so by the fact that he actually had a wry smile on his face.

"Ready?" Melinda asked.

"Ready," Frederick said.

Melinda brought the bundle outside and laid it on the front lawn. Frederick and Wendy followed. The clouds hung low and gray, and the grass was slightly damp from a bit of rain, though the air was clear for the moment. Melinda smelled earth and grass mixed with dusty wool from the blankets.

"Your land," Melinda said. "And you have my word I'll bury this in your grave beside your wife."

"You're no longer trapped," Wendy added.

"But I am," Frederick said sadly. *"I was trapped my entire life, wasn't I? Trapped by my greed and my own self-hatred."* The last of the smallpox rash left his face, leaving it smooth and whole. *"Did Florence tell you I blamed her for my wife's death?"*

"Yes," Melinda said.

"Actually, I didn't," Frederick said. *"I blamed myself. It was because of me that Regina had the baby. If I hadn't . . . touched her, Regina would have been alive. But that was too painful to think about, so I blamed Florence instead. It was easier, and I was a coward. I locked her up on the slightest pretext because looking at her made me think of my own faults, and I couldn't face them. I called Arthur weak because I was too weak to face my own fears. I was a monster, a horrible father, and a filthy excuse for a human being."*

"It's all over now," Melinda said.

"It is, isn't it?" Frederick wiped his eyes on his sleeve and looked down at his own skeleton. *"My imprisonment lasted through life and death, and it all was my own doing. Oh!"* He looked across the yard into the distance. *"Is that . . . is that for me?"*

"Is it a light?" Wendy asked. She let go of the thread and it faded away.

Frederick stared, and a look of absolute wonder came over his face. A bit of his feelings spilled over into Melinda, and her heart filled with a thousand liquid colors.

"It's the most beautiful thing I've ever seen," he said. *"Can I . . . is it . . . ?"*

"Go!" Melinda said. She would have pushed him if it were possible. "You've waited long enough."

Frederick laughed, a bright, cheerful sound that rose far above the clouds to the sun beyond them. *"I can't imagine why I didn't do this eighty years ago. Thank you, dear ladies! Thank you so much."* He laughed again, then turned away from the two women and disappeared.

"Wow," Wendy said in a wistful voice. *"I had no idea it could work that way. Dad never said."*

"I wish there had been a way to prove it to you," Melinda said. "I'm sorry."

There was a sharp noise to Melinda's left. She whirled in time to see the truck door bang open. Jim leaped out, disentangling himself from his blankets like an escaping mummy. All traces of the disease were gone from his face and hands.

"Jim!" Melinda cried, and flew toward him. A moment later, his arms were tight around her and her face was buried in his chest. She inhaled his scent, felt his hand stroking her hair, heard his voice in her ear. Tears of joy and relief rolled down her cheeks, and she felt so happy and light that the faintest breeze would carry her away if Jim weren't holding her.

"Are you all right?" he said. "What happened?"

"I'll explain later," she said. "Just hold me."

He did for a considerable time, and Melinda let herself just rest in the fortress his arms made around her. At last she lifted her face for a kiss, a long one, and then they separated.

"I'm going to need some help with a shovel," she said, "and with explaining to the medical examiner. Can you do that?"

Jim kept an arm around her shoulder. "Once you tell me what's going on. Are those . . . bodies on the front lawn?"

Some of Melinda's earlier happiness leaked away. "Yeah. One under a sheet and one under a blanket."

"Whose?" Jim asked sharply.

Melinda glanced over at the bundles in question. Wendy was standing over her own covered body, looking down at the white-draped shape with an unreadable expression on her face. "One is Wendy King. The other is Frederick Ray."

"Wendy King?" Jim said, shocked. "Oh my God. What happened?"

Melinda was about to explain when the front door banged open. Kevin, Sally, and April burst out of the house and rushed down the porch steps. All three of them were the picture of health.

"Here you are!" Kevin said.

"We searched the house and couldn't find you," Sally added.

"Are you okay, Melinda?" April asked. She looked odd without the music buds in her ears. "I was really sick, I remember that, and I had some bad dreams, and then all of a sudden I was better. Was it real?"

"Partly," Melinda said. "You're all well, then?"

"Perfectly," Kevin said. His red hair was disheveled and his clothes were wrinkled, but he looked fine. "Not even a trace of fever."

Jim flicked a pointed glance over April's head at Wendy's body and at the bundle of blankets, then jerked his head at the house. Wendy gave Jim a wry look, though he couldn't see it.

"Look, why don't you guys go inside and get some tea and cookies going?" Melinda said. "No reason to stand around out here. I'll come in and explain everything in a minute. There's one last thing I need to take care of first."

Sally caught sight of Wendy's covered corpse at that moment and started to ask something, but Jim caught her eye and shook his head sharply. Sally blinked, then nodded.

"Let's go on in," she said. "I think I have a stash of Girl Scout cookies hidden somewhere."

"Are they made with real Girl Scouts?" April asked as they all headed for the front door. Sally and Jim were careful to keep themselves interposed between April and the sad bundles on the front lawn.

"Old joke, old joke," Kevin said, putting a hand on her shoulder. Jim shot Melinda a final glance as they climbed the porch steps, and Melinda mouthed *I love you* to him. He gave a small smile and went inside with the Rays.

"This is so strange," Wendy said, staring down at the sheet that lay over her body.

"Do you see a light?"

Wendy gave a little bark of a laugh. *"It's funny to be on the receiving end of that question. I knew it would have to happen one day. I hardly thought it would be so soon."*

Melinda gave her a small smile. "So what's the answer?"

"You mean, do I see a light? No. Not even the sun. Would you like a ghostly assistant?"

"Don't even," Melinda said, holding up her hands and backing away.

"It was just a joke. My second one, I suppose." Wendy sighed. *"I know why I'm still here, actually. I need to tell you something. Two things."*

"Oh? What?"

"I have . . . difficult news for you, Melinda. Life is always unfair to people with our gifts. Mine ultimately caused my death. Don't cry for me, dear—I didn't have much of a life, and I suspect whatever's waiting for me over there will be much more interesting. In your case, the gift means difficult times are coming. A terrible trial will literally drop upon you

from the sky, and that trial will be just the beginning. But you're strong, stronger than I was. You have the strength to do what needs to be done. There will be pain, but there will also be great rewards."

Melinda found her mouth had gone dry. "Can you tell me more? As in, with details?"

"No, and not because I'm being coy. I can see things now that I'm dead, but the world is strange now. Fuzzy. I can't describe anything better than that because I can't see better than that. I'm sorry."

"All right," Melinda said. "Duly noted. What else did you need to tell me?"

"Just this: thank you."

"For what?"

"For showing me that I was stronger than I thought. For inspiring me to free myself from my father's grip. I know you didn't set out to do it, but you did nonetheless. And you showed me what it's like to help a soul cross over without pain. I got to experience that at least once, and I thank you. I'm sorry I made your life difficult. Can you forgive me for that?"

"Of course," Melinda said. "I only wish we could have met in a different time and place. We might have been good friends."

"Friends." A small tear ran down Wendy's face. There was no sign of the smooth, concrete expression she usually wore. It had been replaced with a mixture of sorrow and relief. *"Thank you for that,*

too. It means more than you know." She turned and looked into the distance.

"Is it . . . ?" Melinda said.

"It is," Wendy said, and the world's widest smile came to her face. Melinda's heart filled for the second time that day. *"Oh, dear. Look at that. I never imagined anything could be so wonderful. Oh, Melinda. This is nothing to be afraid of. I think we spend our whole lives waiting for it. We just don't know it."*

"No need to wait now," Melinda said.

"None at all," Wendy agreed. She turned away from her body and walked with firm steps across the lawn. Then she faded and vanished.

EPILOGUE

"So?" Andrea said. "What happened then?"

"A lot of cleanup," Melinda replied.

It was morning, and bright autumn sunshine poured through the windows of Same As It Never Was. An enormous number of recently acquired antiques were on display, ready for buyers. Andrea and Melinda both stood behind the counter, fragrant cups of Village Java coffee at their elbows. Both of them stared at the front door, waiting.

"We called an ambulance to come for Wendy's body," Melinda said, peeling the top off her cup and taking a sweet sip. "It showed no signs of smallpox. I told the attendants she was helping out at the house and she just collapsed on the way back to her car. It'll probably come back as a heart attack. We hid Frederick's bones, of course, and once the ambulance was gone, Jim and Kevin buried them in the grave he was originally supposed to be in."

"What about the house?" Andrea shot the front door another glance.

"No spirits left in it, if that's what you mean," Melinda said. "But Kevin's putting off the bed-and-breakfast for a while, perhaps indefinitely. He said the spirits are gone, but the memories aren't."

"Yeah, and I can just see the advertisments," Andrea said. She put out her hands as if framing a picture. "Ye Olde Plague Room Special! Ten Percent Off Ye Pox!"

"Shush! We're keeping that part quiet." Melinda took another sip of coffee without taking her eyes off the front door. "All I can say is, thank God he's still selling off the antiques."

"Oh yeah," Andrea said with heartfelt fervor. "Thank God and a whole bunch of minor saints for that. If it weren't for the Ray antiques filling our lovely little store—"

Just then, the front door opened with a jingling of the customer bell. More than a dozen Asian women in pantsuits swarmed into the store.

"There it is," Andrea said. "Right on time."

"This store belong to Melinda Gordon?" one of the women asked.

"You bet," Melinda sang out.

"Good! We talk to Mrs. Xing."

"Of course you did," Andrea said as the other

women spread out across the display floor, oohing and aahing at what they saw. "She seems to have an awful lot of friends."

"Yes," the lead woman said with a firm nod. "She say you have luckiest antiques in three states, so we come. All of us."

"We do love Mrs. Xing," Melinda said. "What's she up to?"

"Getting very deep suntan in Tahiti," the woman said. "How much for these dolls? I want five of them."

"Like you said," Andrea murmured to Melinda, "thank God."

With that, they got to work.

Not sure what to read next?

Visit Pocket Books online at
www.simonsays.com

Reading suggestions for
you and your reading group
New release news
Author appearances
Online chats with your favorite writers
Special offers
Order books online
And much, much more!

POCKET BOOKS
A Division of Simon & Schuster
A CBS COMPANY

POCKET STAR BOOKS
A Division of Simon & Schuster
A CBS COMPANY

13456